STAR

OF SHADOWBROOK FARM

STAR

OF SHADOWBROOK FARM

Joanna Campbell

Produced by Alloy/17th Street Productions,
151 West 26th Street, New York, New York 10001

Cover illustration: © Paul Casale
Cover layout: Stabenfeldt A/S
Typeset by Roberta L. Melzl
Editor: Bobbie Chase
Printed in Germany, 2008

ISBN: 1-933343-77-X

Stabenfeldt, Inc.
457 North Main Street
Danbury, CT 06811
www.pony4kids.com

Available exclusively through PONY Book Club.

The old clock on the stable office wall chimed four o'clock as Susan Holmes walked in from the barn. It was time to begin the intermediate jumping class she taught. She waved to Kirin O'Brien, one of the hired instructors, whose wiry frame was bent over a filing cabinet drawer. Then Susan strode across the small and cluttered office to collect her hard hat from the shelf.

This was one class Susan didn't enjoy teaching. She'd been riding for most of her fourteen years and loved living and working at her family's stable, but Tara Pendleton was in Susan's next class. Susan and Tara did not get along. They had both just begun ninth grade, but that was about all they had in common. Tara, with her long blond hair and thick-lashed blue eyes, was petite, pretty, and the most popular girl in class. Susan was five feet nine and skinny, and felt plain and painfully shy when she was away from horses and the farm. Just looking at Tara made Susan feel like an overgrown giant, but it was Tara's personality that really got to her. Tara had been obnoxious in the eighth grade but was unbearable in ninth, since all the boys had started paying tons of attention to her.

Susan jammed her hard hat over her straight, thick, shoulder-length brown hair. She never knew what to do with her hair, so she usually wore it pulled back into a stark ponytail. She jumped as Kirin gave an exasperated cry from across the room. "Furball!" Kirin yelled, swinging her hand over the battered desktop in the corner. "Look at the mess you've made of these papers! You've gotten paw prints all over them!"

A very large and very furry gray tiger cat leisurely jumped from the desk and came over to rub against Susan's long legs. Susan bent down to pat the cat as Kirin glared at them and ran her fingers through her already unruly mop of curly black hair.

"They're only bills," Susan said.

"Your father's not going to like it," Kirin answered.

"He won't care as long as they're not entrance forms."

"Furball knows the difference, don't you, boy?"

The cat purred loudly as Joany Gretsky, the stable's other instructor, came through the door from the stable. "Your class is all set," she said to Susan. "I had Micky saddle Jocko for you." Joany leaned her shoulder against the doorjamb. She was solidly built and as blond as Kirin was dark. Both girls were in their twenties and from the nearby small town of Norbridge, Connecticut. They were both aspiring three-day eventers and taught at Shadowbrook Farm in exchange for a small salary, free board for their horses, and the use of the farm's training facilities.

"Thanks." Susan gave the cat a last pat and stood. "Did everyone show up?" She was hoping against hope that Tara had suddenly come down with some highly lethal virus and was confined to bed. But no such luck.

Joany nodded. "They're all here."

Susan straightened her shoulders and went out into the bright September sunshine, bracing herself for an hour with Miss Know-it-all. In front of her was the wide, graveled drive and yard area. Her family's old colonial farmhouse was just visible through the trees. To Susan's left was the outdoor schooling ring, and behind her the old red barn with its new stable-wing addition. Beyond that was the even newer indoor ring, which her parents had saved for years to build. Surrounding it all were fifty acres of pasture and woodland and cross-country trails.

The students in Susan's intermediate class were lined up with their horses, ready to go into the schooling ring. Tara was looking bright and perky in new white breeches with her blond hair in a long, feminine French braid down her back. Susan collected her own mount, a lanky bay hunter, from the railing in front of the stable where he was tied, and swung into the English saddle. Jocko was a new acquisition. He was green and only partially trained – not ready to be given to any of the students as a mount. Susan didn't always ride when she taught a lesson, but the new horse needed exercise and exposure to the schooling ring.

There were six students, both boys and girls, in Susan's class, all in their teens or slightly younger. They rode stable-owned jumpers. Susan liked everyone in the class, with the exception of Tara. All the students knew basic equitation and had been jumping for several months, although some were better and more confident than others. Tara was the most confident of all, of course.

Susan gathered the reins and urged her horse forward. "Okay, into the ring," she called.

The students led their mounts into the huge, fenced oval where a variety of jumps had been set up on the well-worked dirt. As usual Tara led the way. She gracefully swung into the saddle of the copper-coated chestnut she usually rode. Her head was tilted arrogantly, and there was a tiny scowl on her face. Apparently she didn't like it when Susan taught the class, probably because she didn't like to admit Susan was the better rider. But riding was the one thing Susan knew she was good at. When she was in the saddle she felt completely confident, just the opposite of the shy, awkward nobody she was at school.

When the class was mounted and ready, Susan called, "Start walking them." Susan walked Jocko along inside the class as they circled the ring outside the jumps. The horse didn't want to settle down. He fidgeted beneath her and was distracted by the other horses, but Susan had ridden worse. "Take it easy," she told him quietly, then raised her voice to call to the class, "Trot them."

The warm-up was important; the horses needed to be limbered before being asked to jump. Susan posted comfortably to Jocko's trot, lifting her weight when he lifted his outside shoulder, but her mind wasn't entirely on what she was doing. Watching Tara made her think of how much she hated school that year. Her best, and only, friend, Dianna Parker, had moved to California, and you couldn't get much farther than that from Litchfield County, Connecticut! Now Susan had no one to talk to, no one to sit with at lunch except kids who had nothing in common with her. She definitely wasn't one of the popular crowd – she really wasn't part of any crowd, for that matter.

Susan automatically gave the class the command to canter. She circled Jocko twice, forcing him with the firm pressure of her legs and hands to concentrate on what he was doing. Then she brought him to the center of the ring and stopped him as she watched the students. She wouldn't be taking Jocko over any of the jumps. If his behavior today was any example, he'd need a lot more time getting used to the schooling ring. When the students had finished three laps, she motioned them to stop and join her at the head of the ring.

"Today we're going to start with some gymnastics," she told them. She pointed to the combination of five jumps set up on one side of the ring. The series started with a low crossbar, then went to horizontal jumps, each progressively higher than the last.

"I was wondering when we were going to try these," Tara said. "I saw Joany using them with her intermediate class weeks ago."

Susan ignored her. "Trot to the cross in your jump seat," she instructed the class. "The rhythm is going to be jump, land, squeeze with your legs, jump, land, squeeze. You have to keep your momentum up – otherwise you're going to get a refusal. Marcy, you start." Susan nodded to a slight, dark-haired girl. She noticed Tara's frown over having to wait, but the other kids needed more help than Tara. Marcy trotted around the end of the oval ring toward the cross bar. She comfortably cleared the first three jumps; then her mount stopped and refused the fourth jump.

"More leg," Susan told her. "Let him feel the pressure.

9

Take him around and start again." This time as Marcy came through the series, Susan coached her between each jump, calling, "Squeeze . . . squeeze . . . squeeze . . ." Marcy and the horse she was riding went through cleanly, and the girl was beaming as she circled the horse and pulled him up. "Good," Susan told her. "Okay, Tim."

She repeated the process until every member of the class had gone through cleanly. Tara had succeeded on her first try and was looking pretty pleased with herself.

"We're going to add another jump," Susan said. "Go through the combination, come around the end of the ring, and jump the brush." Susan pointed to the moderate-size brush on the opposite side of the ring. "Judge your approach carefully."

Tara had positioned herself to go first. From the nervous expressions on the faces of the other students, Susan could see none of them was eager to start. She shrugged. "All right, Tara, go ahead."

Tara went through brilliantly, but she already had such a swelled head, Susan almost hated giving her praise. The rest of the class, though, were having problems – misjudging strides, losing their momentum, getting refusals – especially after Susan added another fence to the course.

Tara was the only one to go entirely clean. Everyone else had trouble with their pacing on the last two fences. "You'll have to give them more leg," Tara butted in when Marcy and Tim completed their circuits. "You're putting in too many strides before the jump."

Susan was trying to explain something to one of the younger students who'd yet to try the extended course, but when she heard Tara, she swung her head around. "Marcy's mount is smaller than yours, Tara. He needs the extra strides. You did fine, Marcy. You just need to keep after him a little more. Monty gets lazy. Keep your head up and your eyes ahead. Don't relax until you're over the last fence."

"Tim's horse doesn't need the extra," Tara snipped.

"No," Susan gritted her teeth. "Watchman can do it in five. Keep your leg on him, Tim. You judged the second fence perfectly. It's harder judging the brush since you're circling toward it around the end of the ring."

Tara was smiling in satisfaction, even if she was only half right.

Susan sent the last two students off, but they both seemed confused now, and Tara didn't help with her under-voiced comments to them about how the course should be ridden. Susan was rapidly losing her temper, especially when Jennifer, looking totally lost, popped her horse over the brush, landed completely off balance, lost her reins, and was nearly thrown from the saddle. Fortunately the horse stopped. Jennifer was all right and quickly sat back and gathered the reins, but she looked like she was ready to cry in frustration.

"You should have gotten after him," Tara cried.

At that, Susan absolutely lost it. "Tara, I'm teaching this class. Will you please butt out!" She was so angry, she wasn't thinking straight. She gathered up Jocko's reins. "Jennifer, take Autumn over to the side. Now watch me – count my strides. As soon as you're out of the combination, look ahead to the brush. When you're over the brush, look ahead to the gate. Head up all the time. Jumping isn't all mechanical. You have to learn how to feel it too – learn to know when you've hit the right takeoff point." She wasn't about to let Tara start taking over the class. She could show her!

In her fury with Tara, she'd completely forgotten she was on a green horse.

Jocko's ears pricked as soon as Susan put him into a trot. She settled into her jump seat and headed the horse around the top of the ring. She'd ridden this course so many times, it was second nature. The first low X went cleanly . . . land, squeeze, jump. But before she was halfway through, she knew she was going to have trouble. Jocko was overexcited, and the course was well beyond his experience. He was panicking, trying to rush through, barely lifting high enough to clear the rails. But Susan was too angry to stop him and lose face. It wasn't going to be easy, but she was sure her knowledge and experience would get them through.

They came out of the combination, but Jocko had twisted his hindquarters going over and landed awkwardly. Susan was flung up on his neck, and a precious inch of rein slipped through her fingers. Instantly she settled and tried to collect the horse, but her momentary lack of control was all the overexcited horse needed. He thrust his head forward, taking the extra rein, and bolted.

Now Susan made every effort to stop him, sitting back, sawing on the reins, but the horse was beyond listening. Desperately she hauled on his inside rein, trying to circle him until he calmed down. But Jocko was galloping now, out of control. He saw the brush jump ahead and bolted toward it instinctively. The confused horse had been taught to jump, and he was doing it.

The next moments were a nightmare. Everything was

happening so quickly, and yet it seemed to Susan that they were moving in slow motion. For the first time in her life Susan knew the horror of being on a horse totally out of control. She didn't have time to think about the fact that her class was watching. She just prayed she could get him back in control.

They sailed over the brush, but Jocko lunged forward after landing, came up to the wall a half-stride off, and popped over like a crazed jackrabbit, nearly unseating Susan. She lost a stirrup and thought fleetingly that this could only end in disaster. She tried to sit up and haul back on the reins, but Jocko surged straight forward again, ignoring her pressure on the reins. Without her stirrup, Susan was handicapped. He was headed right for the schooling-ring fence.

No, Susan thought in terror. *We'll never make it!* The fence was too high – much higher than any of the jumps. And it was built of heavy wooden boards. They could both be hurt – or worse – if Jocko didn't clear that fence. She knew it was hopeless, but she tried to give him all the help she could. It was her fault for taking a green horse over that course. Jocko gathered himself to jump, and Susan squeezed hard with her legs. It wasn't enough.

She knew what was going to happen even before his hind legs crashed into the top fence board. The next moment she was flung forward like a rag doll, over Jocko's head, spinning through the air. The ground rushed up. Susan landed with a jarring crunch and looked up in horror to see a thousand pounds of horse coming down toward her. Jocko's front legs curled under him as he landed, just missing her. Then he fell to his side, trapping Susan's arm

13

beneath him and colliding with her body, knocking every ounce of breath from her lungs.

Susan must have blacked out for a second. When she came to, she was stunned; she couldn't breathe. She couldn't move. A low groaning, gasping noise was all that escaped her lips. Susan struggled to draw air into her lungs and became aware of pain, in her arm, in her side. Through half-focused eyes she saw the horse had righted himself. Someone had grabbed his reins and was leading him away. At least he hadn't broken a leg. Then she saw faces leaning over her, heard Tara's sharp command, "Marcy, go get help. Don't move," she added to Susan.

Moving was impossible anyway, but Susan's mind was beginning to register the humiliation. Her whole class stared down at her with wide and frightened eyes . . . except Tara, who looked completely in control of the situation. Susan understood what it must have looked like to them – she, the instructor, had been totally unable to control the horse she was riding, taking it over the same course Tara had finished perfectly. No one would be thinking about Jocko being a green horse – besides, she should have known better than to put him over those fences! She had set the worst possible example and had probably injured a horse in the bargain. If only the ground would open up and swallow her.

Then she heard her father's and mother's voices. "Get back," they said to the class members. "Give her room." Her mother knelt beside her. "What happened?" she asked. Susan could only weakly shake her head. She was in too much pain to speak.

Her father was frowning worriedly. "Have you broken anything? What hurts?"

14

"My . . . my arm . . . or wrist," Susan gasped softly. "And here . . . " She touched her right side and immediately winced in agony.

"Broken ribs, maybe," her mother said. "Kirin, call an ambulance. Okay, just lie still," she added to Susan. "Somebody get a blanket."

"I already did." Tara handed a clean horse blanket to Mrs. Holmes.

"Good thinking," Mrs. Holmes told her.

Susan closed her eyes. She couldn't stand to see Tara's face and know what Tara was thinking. Riding was the only thing Susan did well, and now she'd royally messed up in front of the one person who would never let her forget it!

She kept her eyes squeezed shut until she heard the ambulance siren.

"A few days' rest and you'll be back on your feet again," Susan's mother said that evening as she sat on the edge of Susan's bed. Mr. Holmes stood behind her, looking upset. Susan's wrist was in a cast. It was fractured, the doctor had said. Her ribs, fortunately, had been only badly bruised, not broken. Every inch of her throbbed and ached, but it was the blow to her pride that hurt the worst.

"What happened exactly?" her father asked.

Susan had been too shaken at the hospital to talk. She wished she didn't have to explain now, either, but she did, haltingly, feeling her parents' eyes boring into her. She omitted the part about getting angry with Tara and trying to show her up. "I just wasn't thinking," she mumbled. "I forgot he was green. I wanted to demonstrate to the class. I know I shouldn't have jumped him … " she finished lamely.

"No, you shouldn't have," Mr. Holmes said. He straightened his tall frame and sighed. Both her parents were tall, although Susan had her father's brown hair, blue eyes, and strong-boned features, while her mother was

16

fair, with short, lightly curling blond hair and hazel eyes. "But you've learned something. You won't do it again. Thankfully, no one in the class panicked and got hurt."

"No," Susan murmured, feeling like she'd let her parents down too. They trusted her to be safety conscious. There was always a chance of a student getting injured, without her causing an unnecessary accident. How could she have been so dumb? Why hadn't she been thinking? She knew, of course. It was all because she'd wanted to put Tara in her place. "How's Jocko?" she asked.

"He'll be okay," her father answered. "He's bruised where he rapped the fence, but he didn't do any serious damage to himself. He should be all right in a few days. You're in a lot worse shape."

"The doctor wants you to stay quiet for a week and give your ribs a chance to heal," her mother said. "I'll call the school and explain and get any makeup work you'll need."

Susan nodded, then closed her eyes, trying to block out the memory of her fall.

Her mother gently patted Susan's hand. "You rest. I'll bring you something to eat in a little while."

Susan watched them leave the room, then let out a long, groaning sigh. At least she didn't have to go to school for a few days. She was too mortified to face Tara. It would be worse than ever now. Norbridge Regional Middle School wasn't very big to begin with, and Tara would have spread around the story of Susan's fall, probably gloating to her friends about how well she'd ridden the course herself. Susan had felt out of it before – after Tara got through, she'd really seem like a gawky, oversize loser.

A tear slid down her cheek. Oh, why did Dianna have

17

to move away? If she were here now, Susan thought, at least she'd have someone to talk to. Dianna had always been chubby and self-conscious about her weight, her thick glasses, and her mouthful of braces. She knew what it was like not to be one of the popular crowd – not to be popular at all. Like Susan's, Dianna's best friends were horses, and her riding skill was the thing she was most proud of. She would understand exactly how Susan felt messing up so badly in front of Tara Pendleton and the rest of her riding class.

In the morning Susan didn't feel any better. She hadn't slept well, waking up again and again from dreams of her accident – that horrifying moment when she knew she and Jocko weren't going to clear the fence … her feeling of panicked helplessness, waiting for the disaster she couldn't prevent … then falling with a sickening crash and looking up to see a thousand pounds of horse coming down toward her.

The dreams left her shaking and sick. Never before had she had such a terrible fall, or been so frightened afterward. She wanted to blot it all out, never think of it again, but she couldn't. Every time she moved and discovered a new ache, she was reminded. But the worst ache was inside. What did her class and everyone else at the stable think of her now?

She could only pick at her breakfast, and when Kirin and Joany came by late in the morning to see her, she was so embarrassed, she could barely look them in the eye.

"You really did a number on yourself," Kirin said, shaking her head. "But you'll be back in the saddle in no time."

"Jocko isn't too bad for the fall," Joany added with a comforting smile. "He's bruised and sore, but otherwise okay."

"I should never have taken him over the course," Susan said miserably. "I don't know what I was thinking of."

"When you're trying to make a point to the class, it's easy to forget you're on a green horse." Kirin thoughtfully narrowed her bright blue eyes. "I'll take him out in a couple of days and give him a good schooling. He needs it. And don't worry about your classes. Joany and I will split them up between us."

"Are you sure? That's a lot of extra work for you. You're trying to get Charming ready for Ledyard." Ledyard was the most prestigious horse trial in New England and was less than a month away. Susan knew how important it was to both Kirin and Joany.

"We'll make it. He's coming along really well. Just get better."

Late that afternoon her mother came into the bedroom with a pile of books. "Tara brought these over," she said with a smile. "She got your next week's assignments from your teachers. That was nice of her, wasn't it?"

Susan made a noise in her throat. Her mother didn't seem to notice as she set the books down on the night table, but Susan knew Tara's motive wasn't sincere. She'd probably made a big production out of getting the assignments, making sure everyone knew what a klutz Susan was.

"Do you want me to bring you juice or anything?" Her mother asked.

"No, thanks, I'm fine."

"You hardly ate any lunch." Her mother frowned. "You've got to eat. You're so thin already."

Skinny was more like it, Susan thought, but she wasn't hungry. "I'm fine, Mom."

"All right. I'll be in the den if you need me. I have some paperwork to do."

Not until the next night at dinnertime did Susan get out of bed. Miserable as she was, she was getting bored, and when she lay in bed, all she did was think about the accident – and that was the last thing she wanted to do. Her first few steps were torture, though, and when she changed her nightgown and took a good look at her side and legs, she saw they were purpled with livid, ugly bruises. Even the side of her face was discolored. She knew she was lucky she hadn't fractured more than her wrist.

She gingerly walked downstairs and arrived in the kitchen just as her father and her older brother, Lyle, came in through the back door. Lyle, tall, with thick brown hair and blue eyes, looked like a younger version of their father. He had just arrived home from college. It was the first weekend he'd been home in the three weeks since the fall semester at the University of Connecticut had begun.

For a second Susan forgot her own troubles, and gave Lyle a big grin. She'd idolized him for as long as she could remember and had tagged around on his heels when she was little. She'd clung to him so often, avidly watching him ride and train for shows, that he'd started calling her Brat. Even though he was now a senior in college studying to be a vet, Lyle still competed with his two horses, Sir George and Hijinx. Now the only time he had to train them was on free weekends when he made the trip home from Storrs in his battered old car.

Lyle gave Susan a big smile in return. "How's it going, Brat?" Then he took a good look at her and whistled. "Wow, you took some kind of a spill, didn't you? Dad was telling me, but I didn't think you'd look this bad. You hurting?"

"I'm pretty sore."

"Pretty dumb taking that horse over the jumps," Lyle added bluntly. "What were you thinking about?"

Susan's smile vanished. She looked down at her feet. "I don't know."

"You're lucky you weren't hurt worse, and you could have injured the horse, too."

"You don't have to remind me," she groaned. Lyle's criticism made her want to crawl into a hole.

"It would have been different if you'd been on a schooled horse. Everybody takes a spill, but to take a crazy risk like you did . . . I've never known you to be so dippy –"

Susan couldn't take any more. She burst into tears, then turned and stumbled up the stairs to her bedroom. She slammed the door behind her with her uninjured hand and flung herself down on her bed. Her bruised ribs protested, but she was already so miserable, she didn't even flinch.

A few minutes later her mother came into the room and knelt by the bed. "Don't cry, sweetheart. You know Lyle always talks before he thinks."

"But he's right," Susan sobbed.

"And you know you made a mistake and won't do it again. Everyone's entitled to a few mistakes."

Susan just shook her head against the pillow.

Susan stayed inside the house for the next several days. She was bored and miserable, but she couldn't face the thought of going to the stables and seeing any of the staff or students. She didn't want any questions or, worse yet, looks of pity. But on Thursday afternoon, a week after Susan's fall, her mother cornered her in the kitchen and handed her her jacket.

21

"You're not doing anyone any good moping around inside. Get out for a while. It's a beautiful day. Go visit the horses or talk to Kirin and Joany. Watch some of the classes."

That was the last thing Susan wanted to do, especially since Tara had a lesson today. "I'm not feeling that great," Susan protested.

"You'll feel better after you get some fresh air," her mother said stubbornly. "Go look at that new hunter your father's training." She draped Susan's jacket over her shoulders. Susan realized she had no choice and went out through the back door of the kitchen, but her steps were leaden as she walked up the drive. If she had to be out, she'd go see the horses. She'd missed them. With Dianna gone, they were her only friends. The one thing she would avoid was the schooling ring, although she had to pass it to get to the barn.

The leaves on the maples overhead were starting to turn brilliant red and orange, but the bright display of color didn't affect Susan's mood. She kicked a pebble with the toe of her shoe and looked straight ahead toward the weathered red barn.

Kirin's voice, loudly calling instructions to the class in the ring, floated through the air. As Susan rounded an overgrown clump of rhododendrons that bordered the drive, she couldn't stop herself from glancing quickly toward the ring.

Tara was taking Jocko over a perfect round of jumps. Susan froze in her tracks and stared. The horse was performing like a lamb for Tara. The jumps weren't difficult, but Susan couldn't believe this was the same horse that had run off with *her*!

All the blood drained from her face, then flooded back in a ruby flush as Tara finished the round and saw Susan standing there.

Tara gave Susan a superior smile and lifted one hand to wave. "He's behaving much better now," she called airily. "He just needed a little work and the right handling." She patted Jocko's neck. The other members of the class had turned to look at Susan, too.

She couldn't stand it. Kirin started to say something, but Susan was already rushing off. At any second she was going to cry, and she fled around the barn, toward the fenced pastures behind. Old stone walls marked the boundaries of the farm. She followed one that separated the farm from the huge Wertheimer Estate. She didn't care where she was going – she wanted only to put as much distance between herself and the schooling ring as possible. Behind the grazing pastures the Holmeses had built a cross-country course of rustic but solid log fences, ditches, spreads, banks, and water jumps that threaded through the woods. They used them in training for the cross-country endurance tests that were part of all horse trials and three-day events.

Susan followed one leg of the course, walking on until her injured ribs began to ache and she had to lean against a tree to catch her breath. Tears stung her eyes and she tried to blink them back. She couldn't believe it. Why had Kirin let Tara ride Jocko? The look on Tara's face! Susan felt betrayed – like someone was twisting a knife in her raw wound.

Suddenly she heard the sound of a voice from somewhere nearby. Had someone followed her? Quickly she looked back along the path she'd followed. She didn't want anyone to see her like this. No one was approaching. In the other direction, across the stone wall bordering the farm, she saw a horse and rider cantering across the neighboring meadow.

The horse was a big, beautifully conformed dapple gray. Susan edged closer through the trees to watch. The horse had a smooth and powerful stride. His muscles rippled beneath his coat, and his dark gray mane and tail flew out behind. One look was enough to tell Susan the horse had good breeding.

As horse and rider drew closer, she recognized the rider as Maxine Wertheimer, the seventeen-year-old daughter of the Holmeses' very wealthy neighbors. Susan didn't know Maxine except by sight; the only time Susan ran into her was at local shows and horse trials, where Maxine excelled. Maxine went to private school and socialized with the country club/hunt club set. Susan had heard plenty about her. She was one of the top riders in New England, but she was also a spoiled brat, used to getting exactly what she wanted. She could be obnoxious at shows when things didn't go her way, and she'd always reminded Susan of an older version of Tara, except that Tara wasn't rich.

It was the horse that held Susan's attention, though. As Maxine cantered him over the grass, Susan pushed a branch out of her line of vision to watch. The two were approaching a log barricade set up at the far side of a narrow brook that ran across the Wertheimers' meadow, then on to the Holmeses' property. Susan knew Maxine must be preparing for the big Ledyard Horse Trials, but she'd never seen her ride this horse before, and she doubted Maxine would ride

24

an untried horse over the grueling Ledyard course. He must be a new addition to Maxine's stable.

The horse and rider headed toward the jump. Maxine rode her horses hard, and she was riding the gray hard now. There was lathered sweat on the horse's coat from a heavy workout. Maxine's seat was perfect as she cantered the horse forward. The gray moved flawlessly – until he saw the flash and sparkle of the water in front of the jump. He started and shied out severely, refusing to go nearer. Maxine instantly lifted her crop and smacked his rump hard, then turned him and approached the jump again.

Again the gray shied, and this time he nearly unseated Maxine. Susan saw Maxine's face tighten with anger. She smacked the horse again and turned him for another try. The horse was huffing and prancing, and flicked his ears backward and forward in fear, but Maxine wasn't giving up. She headed him toward the jump. This time he stopped dead in his tracks. Maxine only saved herself from going over his head by grabbing handfuls of his mane. Angry red blotches discolored her cheeks, and she swore at the horse. She brought her whip down repeatedly on his rump while holding his reins firmly so he couldn't bolt. The horse whinnied shrilly and was trembling as Maxine turned him for yet another try. Lather rimmed his mouth.

Susan slammed her left hand furiously against a tree trunk. This was no way to treat that beautiful horse, unless Maxine was set on ruining him for life! He was obviously inexperienced and hadn't jumped water before. Many horses had a natural fear of jumping water. Maxine should have jumped him over the brook alone first, to let him learn there was nothing to fear.

This time Maxine dug her knees into the horse's sides and hit him hard as they reached the takeoff point. In desperation he jumped – a strong but awkward leap. He landed off balance and stumbled. Quickly, he gathered his legs beneath him and cantered on, but Susan knew he could just as easily have been hurt. She clenched her teeth angrily when she saw the satisfied smile on Maxine's face as she turned the horse. The gray, on the other hand, looked frankly terrified. Maxine didn't deserve a horse like that.

Suddenly Susan's plaster-encased wrist twinged with pain. She looked down at her arm and was sharply and unpleasantly reminded of why it ached. Every horrifying, frightening detail of her fall flashed through her mind. Then she thought of seeing Tara handling the same horse so perfectly minutes before. She squeezed her eyes shut against the image.

"Who am I to talk?" she whispered bitterly. "I'm the idiot who rode a green horse over a too difficult course and let him get out of control!"

When she looked up, Maxine and the gray were cantering off around a bank of trees. Susan shivered and hugged herself. It had suddenly gotten cooler, and she was chilled to the bone. She didn't want to go home, but she didn't want to stay in the woods any longer either. Slowly she turned and started back to the farm. At least Tara would have left by now.

On Monday afternoon the bus dropped Susan off at the end of the farm drive, but her shoulders were slumped as she scuffed along the gravel. Her first day back at school had been about as awful as she'd expected. She had managed to avoid Tara all morning, but Tara had come up to her while Susan was standing in the lunch line.

"Hope you're feeling better," Tara had said sweetly, eyeing Susan's fading bruises and the plaster on her wrist.

Susan knew Tara didn't care whether she was feeling better or not. She was just putting on a show for her snotty friends, who were sitting at a nearby table. Susan could feel them all staring at her. "I'm fine," Susan said shortly, moving ahead with the line.

Tara followed. "It was pretty scary for all of us . . . I mean, seeing the way Jocko took off with you and you couldn't stop him." She smiled.

Susan flung a sandwich on her tray, stopping herself just in time from throwing it in Tara's face. "He was green," she began in self-defense, then stopped. That was a stupid thing to say. It only made her look worse, since she should have known better than to jump a green horse. Her cheeks felt hot, and she knew they were bright red.

"He'll be nice and calm the next time you ride him. The two of us have been doing great," Tara said. "Well, hurry up and get better. See ya." She smiled insincerely and walked away.

Susan's eyes were stinging as she paid for her lunch. She didn't dare look anywhere, but she heard the giggles at Tara's table. She hated them all!

Her day hadn't gotten any better. After missing a week of classes, Susan was totally lost in algebra. There'd been a surprise history quiz, which she'd flunked. By the end of the day she felt so miserable that she wanted to die.

At home there wasn't much to look forward to either. Susan still couldn't do much around the stables, she couldn't ride – not that she really wanted to – and she wasn't about to start teaching any classes again. How could she stand up in front of a group of students with any confidence?

As she approached the house, Susan saw a horse van pulled up in the drive near the stables. Her father was backing a big dapple-gray horse down the ramp and onto the drive. Mrs. Holmes and Kirin were standing nearby, watching as Mr. Holmes circled the horse on the drive. The tall, sleek animal was obviously nervous and unsettled. He flared his delicate nostrils, flicked his ears repeatedly, and snorted as he danced on slender legs and eyed his new surroundings.

Susan started forward with her eyes glued to the big gray. She knew this horse, she was sure of it. This was the horse Maxine Wertheimer had been riding and treating so badly. But why was he here? The Wertheimers would never send a horse to her parents for training, even though the Holmeses were experts.

Susan hurried over and stopped beside her mother and Kirin.

"Nate Wertheimer called me this morning," Mr. Holmes was explaining. "His daughter was training this guy, and he wasn't working out. He wanted to get rid of him and thought he'd make a good stable horse."

A stable horse! Susan had seen him in action and knew he had more talent than that.

"Wertheimer offered to sell him to us cheap. I took the van over there to look at him and liked what I saw." Mr. Holmes shrugged. "So we've got ourselves another horse."

"He looks like a Thoroughbred," Mrs. Holmes said.

"He is. After I saw him, I knew it was too good a deal to pass up. He may have some personality problems if Wertheimer's daughter was having so much trouble with him, but he should be worth the effort, considering how little I paid for him."

Susan muttered angrily under her breath, then quickly stopped when her parents and Kirin turned to look at her.

Susan glanced down. Something stopped her from describing the scene she'd viewed from the woods. She was glad the gray was safe from Maxine's ill treatment, but that was all she could feel at the moment. She was too upset to feel any excitement, and she didn't want to get close to the gray herself.

Kirin walked over and laid a hand on the nervous horse's shoulder. "Do you know anything about his background?" she asked.

"Wertheimer told me he bought him privately in Virginia. He's a four-year-old. At one point he'd been in training for flat racing, then got sold for retraining as a jumper. Beyond that, I don't know much."

"What's his name?"

"Evening Star."

The name fits him, Susan thought. She glanced up to find both her parents looking at her. Looking at the horse, Susan suddenly felt panic at the thought of riding him. All she could see were crashed fences and herself hurtling through the air. Her reaction startled her.

"I've got homework to do," she said, grasping at the first excuse that came to mind. Turning on her heel, she hurried toward the house. When she was safely inside, she leaned back against the closed door and let out a ragged breath. Her hands felt like ice, and her knees were trembling. Then she realized what was wrong. She was afraid – scared to death at the thought of getting in the saddle, especially on another green horse. She'd lost her nerve!

She'd seen it happen with students who'd had a scare or a spill. They couldn't forget. They thought only of the danger, not the thrills and the challenge. They were tense and rigid in the saddle, if they didn't quit riding all together. Susan had never understood before – she'd thought they were cowards. But she understood now.

Numbly Susan walked across the room toward the stairs. This couldn't be happening to her, but the hollow pit in her stomach told her it was. She tried to take her mind off it by attacking her homework but ended up staring at the page, reading the same question over and over. Finally she got up and went down to the kitchen for a glass of milk. As she drank it, she looked out the kitchen window and watched students arriving and departing from lessons. Some of them had been her students. This feeling would go away. It *had* to go away.

That night she started a letter to Dianna. Halfway through she ripped it up and threw it in her wastepaper basket. She couldn't explain the way she felt on paper, even to her best friend. Words couldn't describe how terrified she'd been losing control of a horse, knowing there was going to be a disaster – or how she felt now, knowing she might have lost the nerve to do the one thing she did well.

She buried her face in her hands, then got up and went outside. She was sick of her bedroom, sick of the house. The barn and stables were the place where she'd always felt happiest, and it would be quiet. Her parents were in the den, talking. Kirin and Joany had gone home, and no students would be around. The familiar scents of fresh hay, horse, and leather greeted her as she stepped inside the old, original part of the barn. Huge dark beams rose to the loft, and only dim bulbs lit the interior. A few horses stamped restlessly in their stalls. Others whickered softly. Furball immediately jumped down from a bale of hay in the corner and trotted over to rub his fat body against Susan's ankles. She kneeled to pet him and he purred. The two other stable cats, Ralph and Puss, peeked out sleepily from the tack room at the end of the barn, but they were true barn cats, wary of people.

Furball decided he'd had enough and trotted off down the aisle, tail high. Three quarters of the way down he stopped and sprang nimbly up onto the edge of one of the stall doors. There he sat, perfectly balanced on the narrow perch, and began to wash his face. A moment later Evening Star's sleek gray head appeared over the stall door. He whuffed at the cat, who ignored him and continued preening. Then the horse looked curiously up the aisle and saw Susan standing with her back braced against one of the beams. He pricked his ears and stared, sniffing the air, trying to catch Susan's scent. His head was perfectly shaped, she noticed, and there was a bright spark of intelligence in his eyes. She knew he was one of the best animals they'd ever had in the stable, including her parents' and brother's mounts. But she didn't go any closer to his stall. What would be the point of making friends with this horse when she knew she might never have the courage to ride him? She remembered, though, how elegant he'd looked cantering across the field with Maxine. Once again she felt a prick of anger when she thought of how Maxine had handled him. What could Star do with patient and caring training?

As soon as the thought entered her mind, she pushed it away, turned and left the stable, and went back to the house to bed.

In the morning, Susan woke up with a sick feeling of dread at the thought of having to go to school. School was something to be endured.

And now my afternoons won't be great either, she thought as she came out of the shower, dragged on a pair of jeans and a baggy sweater, and carelessly pulled a comb through her straight brown hair. Her jeans were already too short, she noticed as she sat on the bed to put on her sneakers.

Somehow she got through the next few days, even if

they seemed unending. She started helping with light stable chores: filling feed and water buckets, straightening out tack, and bringing the horses that weren't being ridden in from the pasture at night. A couple of high-school girls came in the afternoons to muck stalls. Susan's wrist wasn't strong enough for her to do any of the heavy work, but Kirin and Joany appreciated any help they could get.

Still, it didn't fill enough of Susan's time, and too often she would find herself standing idly in the barn aisle, staring down at the big gray horse's stall. She made no effort to befriend him, but he always seemed to know when she was there and would come to his stall door, sticking his head over. He was beginning to know her by sight, and he was obviously curious about this human who never came close, only watched. His eyes held such welcome that several times Susan almost crossed the aisle to stroke his nose. She stopped herself. The horse was getting plenty of attention. Kirin and Joany took turns grooming him. During the day he was out in the pasture with the other horses. He didn't need Susan to feel welcome at Shadowbrook Farm.

A week after Evening Star arrived at the farm, Mr. Holmes saw Susan leaving the stable office and motioned to her to join him at the ring. "Come and watch this."

She couldn't very well refuse, even though being near the ring didn't bring pleasant memories. At least there wasn't a class in session. Kirin was up on her big bay, Charming, schooling him in preparation for the show-jumping portion of Ledyard, which was now less than a week away.

Susan stopped at the schooling-ring gate beside her father in time to see Charming and Kirin attempt a wide, spread jump. Before they were halfway through, she could see that Charming didn't have enough lift. His front hoofs caught the top rail of the second spread and sent it tumbling down. Very quickly, he stumbled after it, going to his knees, and Kirin went flying over his head.

Susan squeezed her eyes shut. She couldn't watch. She couldn't stand to see another accident!

Then she heard her father call, "You're going to have to get after him more! That's a wide spread. He's really got to extend himself."

Susan opened her eyes to see Kirin standing in front of the horse, brushing off her breeches and straightening her hard hat. She wasn't hurt. Neither was Charming. Kirin walked back to the jump and bent over to replace the lightweight fallen rail. Then she led Charming to the side of the jump and quickly remounted. She put the horse into a canter and circled him to reapproach the spread.

Susan knew she'd overreacted to the fall, but she held her breath anxiously as she watched their approach. Kirin would be giving the horse all the leg she could, squeezing hard on his sides. This time it was enough. They sailed over cleanly.

"Good," Mr. Holmes said.

Susan sighed in relief as they landed, but she tensed again as Kirin continued on over the difficult course. Not only were the jumps varied and of high difficulty, but they were placed at varying distances, with tight angles and approach turns. A few weeks before, Susan would have attempted most of the jumps herself. Now she was cringing just watching, and she waited in dread for the horse to miss clearing another fence or refuse a jump and send Kirin

34

flying again. Neither happened. Horse and rider came through cleanly.

A smiling and breathless Kirin cantered the horse over.

"Nice job," Mr. Holmes said.

"Very nice," Susan added, though she felt breathless herself.

"Thanks," Kirin said, "But I think he needs a little more work on that double gate. He's hesitating. I'm going to run him through again." Kirin trotted off confidently, and Susan wondered how she could be so fearless. But then, Susan had been pretty fearless herself not long before.

"If they can keep up like this, they're going to do well at Ledyard," her father said, squinting his blue eyes as he watched. "I hope I can get Tuxedo to go as well. It's a shame you can't ride this year," he added. "If you hadn't hurt your wrist, I was going to suggest you ride Hijinx. Lyle's been concentrating on Sir George, but it looks like he'll have to ride both of them now, and he doesn't have much time for training when he can only get home on the weekends."

"What about Mom?" Susan asked automatically.

"Someone's got to stay here and watch the farm."

"Oh, right."

"When did the doctor say the cast can come off?" her father asked.

"A couple of weeks, but then I have to wear a plastic brace thing and an Ace bandage." The way Susan felt right now, she didn't care if her wrist ever got better. As long as her wrist was bandaged, she wouldn't have to admit to anyone that she'd lost her nerve.

"Maybe I'd better get your mother to try out that new

horse, then. Everyone else is too busy. Anyway, you're young. You'll heal fast." He gave her a reassuring smile.

When Susan came into the stable office later that afternoon after bringing in the last horse, Kirin and Joany were talking about Tara.

"She's really coming along," Joany said as she reorganized an assortment of crops hanging on the wall. "She's doing great with Jocko. She tells me she wants to get her own mount."

"She's ready," Kirin agreed. Absently she moved Furball off the next day's schedule and ran her finger down the list of classes. "I like the way she's handling Jocko too. There's that late-October show at the Hunt Club. Maybe we should get her to enter. The two of them ought to be ready by then."

Susan bit her lip and stepped back from the office doorway. In three weeks' time Tara had done so well with Jocko that Kirin and Joany thought she should enter a big show? So Tara's bragging wasn't just bragging. If Tara had been riding another horse, maybe it wouldn't have mattered so much. But for Tara to do so well on the horse that Susan hadn't been able to control . . . it was so humiliating!

Susan went back into the barn. Somehow she found herself standing opposite Evening Star's stall. The big gray horse had his head over the door and was watching her with interest. He seemed to sense that she was a friend, even though she'd yet to speak to him or touch him. Furball trotted down the aisle and leaped up to Evening Star's stall door. It was becoming his favorite perch, especially when Susan was around. The horse gently whuffed into the cat's long fur, then looked out at Susan again.

Here's the horse to show Tara up. He'd outshine Jocko any day, but he'd need a better rider than Tara, Susan thought maliciously. *He'd need a very good rider.* Without realizing where her thoughts were leading, she pictured herself on the big gray's back; cantering around the ring heading for a course of jumps . . . Suddenly Susan brought up her hands and covered her eyes. No! All she could see was them crashing through the jump, falling . . . Tara watching and laughing.

Evening Star nickered from across the aisle. Susan shook her head. The horse nickered again, but Susan fled without looking at him and hurried up to the house for dinner.

Mrs. Holmes heard the horse van returning from Ledyard on the following Sunday night and called out to Susan. "They're back!"

Susan came downstairs and followed her mother out of the house to the stable drive. No matter how Susan felt about herself, this was an exciting moment, finding out how the home team had done at the biggest of all New England events.

Kirin was the first out of the van. She was beaming and ran across the yard to hug Mrs. Holmes and Susan. "We took a first in preliminary!" she cried. "I still don't believe it. Charming was on all the way!"

"Congratulations!" Susan and Mrs. Holmes told the excited young woman. A win in the second-most difficult class at Ledyard was quite an accomplishment.

"I thought we'd do okay," Kirin said, "but I didn't think we'd do this well."

"You've worked hard."

Kirin smiled. "And everyone else did great too. Lyle and Joany got seconds in advanced and training."

"On Sir George," Lyle said, shaking his head in disappointment. "I didn't put enough time into Hijinx. If Susan had been able to work him while I was at school, it might have been different. We totally screwed up the cross-country, but Sir George did great."

"I was the only one without a ribbon," Mr. Holmes told them as he came over and hugged his wife and daughter. "Tuxedo came up lame before the show jumping, and I pulled him out."

"Anything serious?" Mrs. Holmes frowned.

"No, I had the show vet look at him. Just a slight sprain. He'll be all right with a compress and a few days' rest. The good news is that we got second in dressage and the high score on cross-country. A real good weekend overall, and a good boost for the farm. I talked to a couple of riders who may be interested in boarding and training here over the winter. Let's get the horses put away and fed. They deserve a good meal tonight!"

Later, when the horses were settled, Lyle immediately set off for his return trip to college. The others gathered in the stable office, and Joany and Kirin excitedly filled Susan in on the gossip and who'd been riding.

"Maxine Wertheimer was there," Joany said as she absently removed the pins that had held her long blond hair in a neat bun for the competition. "She was riding a new horse – a big chestnut Anglo-Arab."

"How'd she do?" Susan couldn't help asking, wondering if Maxine treated her new horse any better than she had Evening Star.

"Third in young open intermediate. Not bad, considering it's their first competition together. But that horse has had plenty of experience. He knew what he was doing."

"Speaking of the Wertheimers," Mr. Holmes said, "what's happening with the horse I bought from them?"

Kirin shrugged. "I haven't ridden him, but he's a real hard horse to get to know. Standoffish. He doesn't like to make friends – won't let anyone get too close."

Susan frowned. She hadn't sensed the horse's unfriendliness at all. But Joany was nodding. "I get the same feeling. He doesn't trust anyone."

Susan could have told them that Maxine had frightened the horse by the way she'd heavy-handled him, but she kept her lips shut. What did it matter to her? She wasn't going to get involved with him anyway.

"We'll give him a little more time," Mr. Holmes said.

That night Susan reread the letter she'd received from Dianna that week, but Dianna's cheery words left her more upset than happy. Dianna loved California, and she went on about her parents' small ranch and a friend she had met at school who went riding with her. After reading the letter, Susan didn't want to confide her own problems anymore. She picked up her pen and wrote a letter in answer, but this time she didn't mention her accident, or her reaction, or her confusion. The letter read more like fiction than fact. Maybe it would have been different if Dianna had been there to talk to face-to-face, but she wasn't.

On Monday morning Susan looked up from her locker to see Tara approaching with several of her friends in tow. Tara stopped and leaned her shoulder against the neighboring locker. "Hey, Susan. Did you hear I'm going to be riding in the Hunt Club show with Jocko?"

"Oh, are you?" Susan tried to sound indifferent.

"You didn't know? Where have you been, hiding? I sure never see you around the stable anymore." Tara said it teasingly, but her words stung.

Susan slammed her locker shut. "I've been busy with other things."

"I guess you can't do much with a broken wrist. Aren't you going to be teaching classes anymore? You could always stick with the beginners." With that Tara sauntered off.

Susan gritted her teeth and ducked her head to hide the embarrassed blush on her cheeks. *Wasn't Tara popular enough? Does she have to put me down too, just to make herself feel good? But I am hiding, aren't I?* she thought miserably.

Susan didn't have much peace at home, either. Her parents started in on her a few days later. "Don't you think it's time you taught a few classes again?" her father said as Susan came into the stable office after cleaning a pile of tack. "It would help take some of the pressure off Kirin and Joany. They've had to double up their duties to take over your classes."

"Ah . . . ah . . ." Susan stuttered, desperately trying to think of any excuse.

Kirin saved her. "Oh, we don't mind," she said. She pushed her black hair out of her face as she strode in from the stable yard. "Let Susan get back on her feet. Besides, Joany loves working with the little kids. She's really good with them, and my schedule isn't all that tight, especially after Ledyard. Charming and I don't have anything big coming up."

Mr. Holmes pulled his reading glasses from his pocket and leaned his long frame back in the desk chair. He studied both girls thoughtfully, then finally shrugged and dropped all four feet of his chair back to the ground. "Okay. I guess we can let things stand for now." He put on his glasses and pulled a pile of bills and feed receipts in front of him. But Susan knew the subject wasn't closed.

She left the office and nearly bumped into her mother, who was in riding clothes and had just led her black Thoroughbred jumper, Passion, to the barn after a work on the cross-country course. Her mother's face was glowing from the exercise, and her blond curls were ruffled. "Oh, Susan, I want to talk to you –"

"Not now, Mom, please," Susan pretended she was in a rush and hurried off toward the pasture. Her mother was going to make the same suggestion; there was no real reason why Susan shouldn't start teaching again. An instructor didn't need to be on horseback to teach a class. Most of the time the instructors were on foot. It had been so easy before. Susan hadn't thought about what she was doing; she'd just done it with confidence. But her fall on Jocko, and Tara's success with him, had changed all that.

"Okay, Furball," Susan said. "That's the last stall finished. Let's go outside for a while before I bring in the horses." It was Sunday afternoon, and the farm was unusually quiet. Kirin and Joany had left for the day. Her parents and Lyle were in the house having a last visit before Lyle left for his return trip to college.

Furball padded after her and rubbed against her legs. Susan absently leaned down to pat him. Her permanent cast had come off earlier in the week, and her wrist was now encased in an Ace bandage over a plastic support. The doctor had said she was healing remarkably fast. *Maybe physically*, she thought, *but not mentally*.

She plucked one of the last blades of grass growing around the barn and chewed it. The middle of October already. Pretty soon all the grass would be brown, the trees bare, and the ground frozen. There'd be snow, too. But that could be fun. Maybe they'd have enough so that her father would hitch up old Domino to the antique sleigh they kept in one of the sheds and take them for a sleigh ride. Domino was big, shaggy, ancient, but still knew how to pull a sleigh. They had an old harness with bells attached. For a moment Susan's face glowed, thinking of all the fun they'd had in the past.

Furball suddenly made a growling noise and walked away from her caressing fingers as a loud whinny pierced the air. Jarred out of her memories, Susan looked out to the pasture. What she saw made her stand up straight.

Evening Star was no longer grazing with the other horses. He'd lifted his head, ears pricked, tail high. Suddenly he took off at a roaring gallop across the pasture. His strides ate up the ground, his every motion fluid. Watching with admiration, she waited for him to stop and turn at the pasture fence – but he didn't! With an extraordinary leap he sailed right over, landed, and galloped off toward the meadows and woods of the cross-country course at the back of the farm.

For an instant Susan was too stunned to move. What a jump! Then her mind registered that they had a horse loose. Star had to be caught. She glanced around frantically, but of course, she was alone. Not thinking beyond that, she ran inside the stable, grabbed a lead shank from the wall, and rushed off in pursuit.

The horse had a good start on her, but there were several acres of meadow he had to cross before he reached the woods. Star's dappled gray body bounded across the last piece of open field; then his hindquarters and flowing tail disappeared as he dashed down one of the cross-country trails. Susan flew after him, not thinking of her fairly recent injuries – only that she had to catch him. At his headlong pace, he could hurt himself, especially if he went beyond the boundaries of the farm.

43

Evening Star was out of sight by the time Susan reached the cross-country course. But the ground was soft from recent rain, and she could clearly see his hoofprints fresh in the mushy earth.

She raced around several of the big log-and-brush barriers on the course – and could see clearly that Evening Star had jumped them. Then suddenly he veered off the course, onto a narrower trail through the woods.

Brush and tree twigs slapped her face as she followed his tracks. He was running randomly now, through openings in the rough woods. Susan yelped as a stray blackberry bramble caught her pant leg, dug through, and cut her skin. She carefully jerked it free, then hurried on. She breathed a sigh of relief when she saw a small clearing ahead and stepped out of the trees just in time to see Evening Star go sailing over one of the rambling stone walls that bordered Shadowbrook Farm and disappear into the distance, into the big estate to the left of the Holmeses' property. It had just been sold. Susan didn't know who lived there now, or if they liked horses.

By the time she scrambled over the stone wall, Susan couldn't see him anymore – he'd headed up the wooded hillside. She searched the ground for tracks, but here the woods were thick and the fallen leaves deep. The ground was totally covered by them, and there were no prints to be seen.

She didn't think of stopping; her parents would have a fit if she did. A loose horse was dangerous to itself and others. Susan thought back to the moments before Star had jumped the paddock fence, wondering what, if anything, had spooked him. She hadn't seen or heard anything – no loud noises. Was he just bored, unhappy, and confused in his new surroundings? After all, no one had really befriended him. Kirin and Joany thought he was standoffish, and they were both too busy to make a real effort with the horse. And Susan hadn't tried to get close to him – just the opposite. She felt a stab of guilt remembering all the welcoming looks he'd given her as he'd gazed over his stall door – and she'd deliberately ignored him.

Calling Star's name, Susan slogged on up the hill, trying to find a clear path through the trees and undergrowth. There was no answering response, no sound of broken branches as he crashed through the wood. As she topped the hill, she was completely surrounded by woodland and was feeling disoriented. Everything around her looked the same. If she could somehow find her way to the neighbor's house, she could call for help, but she didn't know which way to go.

Her heart was pounding from her rapid climb up the steep hill. Her face was scratched from pushing through the brush, her side where she'd bruised her ribs was beginning to ache – and dusk was falling. Susan had to find her way out and find Evening Star before dark, or they'd really be in trouble.

The trees looked slightly less dense to her right, and she thought it was a bit brighter beyond. She set out in that direction. The trees were thinning, and finally she pushed out into an open field. Evening Star was on the far side! He'd stopped his mad dash and was standing with his head raised.

Susan let out a long, relieved sigh. Then she noticed the other horse and rider slowly approaching Star. Susan watched as the rider skillfully maneuvered close to Star, then

45

with a quick movement grabbed the big gray's halter. Star threw up his head in surprise, but the rider held on. Only then did Susan start jogging across the field toward them.

As Susan approached, the rider looked up, saw her, and waited. Susan was close enough to see that the rider was a girl – a very pretty black girl. Actually, the girl was beautiful. She was dressed in riding pants, boots, hard hat, and a bright red, thick-knit sweater, and was riding a nice-looking bay with a white blaze. The girl smiled and called, "Is this guy yours?"

"Yes!" Susan cried breathlessly as she hurried up. "Thank you for catching him. He jumped our pasture fence, and I've been chasing him for at least a half hour." She quickly clipped the lead shank to Evening Star's halter and patted the horse's neck in reassurance. "I'm Susan Holmes from Shadowbrook Farm, next door."

"Whitney Duncan," the other girl said. "We just moved in last week from New York. I'm glad I decided to take Bravo out for a ride."

"Sorry he got loose over here," Susan apologized, as she looked the horse over to see if he'd injured himself. "I hope he didn't get into any trouble."

"Nope. I only saw him when I came off one of the trails, heading home. He was just standing there, and I figured I'd better try to catch him. He's a good-looking horse. Is he yours?"

"My parents'," Susan answered. "We haven't had him long."

"I've only had Bravo a month. I got him when I knew we were definitely moving up here," Whitney said brightly. "Now I'll get a chance to really do some decent riding."

46

"Well, thanks again for catching him," Susan said, glancing around and noticing the fading light. "I'd better get him back before it gets dark."

"You're not going back through the woods, are you?"

"I don't know any other way."

"Go back through our place and take the driveway down to the road." Whitney quickly dismounted and threw the reins over Bravo's head. "Come on. Follow me. Besides, this way we can get to know each other better. You're the first person I've met. We must be about the same age, too. How old are you?"

"Fourteen." But Susan was staring. Now that Whitney had dismounted and was standing beside her, Susan saw that Whitney was as tall as she was!

Whitney didn't notice her stare. She smiled. "Same age as me! This is great! Tell me all about Norbridge," Whitney said as Susan snapped to and started leading Star along beside her. "I've never lived in a small town, but I think it's going to be fun. You must ride too. What happened to your wrist?"

Susan tried to answer Whitney's flow of questions, forgetting her natural shyness for the moment. "I had a fall."

"On him?"

"No, another horse."

"That's too bad. I've had plenty of falls myself. You like living here?"

"Norbridge is an okay place, I guess. I've always lived here. But if you're used to a city, maybe you'll think it's too quiet."

"Oh, I'll get to see plenty of the city," Whitney said.

"My parents will be going down all the time to check on their restaurants. They own a chain of restaurants, though my dad's going to run the business from up here now. And I do some part-time modeling in New York." She gave Susan an appraising glance. "You know, you would make a good model."

"Me?" The last thing Susan could do was picture herself standing and posing in front of a camera. Wouldn't Tara have a laugh over that? "No, I don't think so," she said.

"Why not? You're tall enough and thin enough."

"You mean skinny. No, I'd be much too nervous and I'm not pretty or anything."

"You get used to the cameras, and it's bones that make a good model."

Susan thought of the hollows beneath her prominent cheekbones. She guessed she did have plenty of bones. She felt herself flushing. This conversation was unreal.

Whitney kept chattering on, talking to Susan like they'd known each other for years instead of a few minutes, asking if she had brothers or sisters, telling her she was an only child herself, which she didn't like. Before Susan knew it, they were approaching the Duncan house. She'd never been here before. The former owners, the Prendergasts, hadn't socialized with the Holmeses except at riding events. The house was a huge old white colonial surrounded by ancient trees and set so far back along a winding drive that it couldn't be seen from the road. Behind the house was an immaculate red barn, big garage, sheds, and neatly fenced paddocks. Lush green lawns spread around the front and sides of the house. A BMW and a Jeep Cherokee were parked on the paved drive.

"I really love this place." Whitney sighed. "It was so crowded where we used to live – no open spaces at all! That's one of the reasons we moved here, so I could have a place to keep horses and ride."

Since Susan had lived all her life on a farm in Litchfield County, she didn't have anything to compare it to, except that the Duncan place was an estate, not a farm like theirs. "Do you mind if I call my parents before I go?" she asked. "I think they might be worried by now."

"I was going to ask you to come in anyway," Whitney said. "We can put the horses in the barn. We've got tons of stalls, and only one horse – so far."

Susan had been so enthralled listening to Whitney that she hadn't noticed how calmly and sweetly Star had been following along beside her. Now he gently nudged her with his velvety nose and softly nickered.

"He's glad to be back with you," Whitney said. "He was looking kind of lost when I first spotted him."

Whitney was right. Star was treating her like an old and trusted friend. Susan wasn't sure what to make of it. Without thinking, she rubbed her hand down his neck as she led him into the barn. He whuffed softly in return.

"Put him in there," Whitney motioned to a bedded stall as she untacked Bravo. "There's hay and water at the end of the barn."

Susan led Star into the stall, then collected an armful of hay and a bucket of water. After placing both in the stall, she carefully looked the horse over as he lipped up a mouthful of hay. She hadn't noticed any cuts or scrapes when she'd checked him over in the field, and she saw none now. Star seemed to be in better shape than she was. For several seconds Susan stood quietly watching the horse. Evening Star lifted his head and returned her gaze from warm brown eyes. Was he really unhappy at the farm? she wondered. Again she felt a stab of guilt at ignoring him.

"All set?" Whitney called from the next stall.

"Sure," Susan answered, then lowered her voice. "I'll be back in a little while, boy."

Letting herself out of the stall, she followed Whitney to the house.

"Mom, Pop," Whitney called as soon as they were through the back door into the large and homey country kitchen. Empty packing boxes were still stacked near the door, waiting to be carried outside. "I met a neighbor. Where are you?"

"Yo," a deep voice answered. A moment later Mr. and Mrs. Duncan appeared in the doorway at the other side of the kitchen.

"We were wondering if you'd gotten lost," Mrs. Duncan said with a touch of worry.

"Nope. Everything's fine, and I've even made a new friend. Mom and Pop, meet Susan. She's our neighbor at Shadowbrook Farm. She had a runaway horse." Quickly Whitney explained what had happened. "I didn't want her to have to take him back through the woods."

"Good heavens, no. It's pitch dark out." Mrs. Duncan gave Susan a warm smile. She was as tall and slender as Whitney and just as pretty. "Nice to meet you, Susan."

Mr. Duncan was stockier and looked like he enjoyed a good meal, which would make sense if he owned a chain of restaurants. He stepped forward and shook Susan's hand. "I'm glad Whitney came along to help you out – and glad she's had a chance to meet someone already. It's hard moving into a new area, though I guess you've noticed that Whitney isn't exactly shy."

Susan smiled. "I noticed."

"How about a drink and snack?" Mrs. Duncan offered.

"If you don't mind, I'd like to use the phone to call my parents."

"Of course! It's right over there on the desk." Mrs. Duncan motioned to an old rolltop desk, above which were shelves of cookbooks.

"I'll get some sodas and cookies," Whitney said, gliding off to the refrigerator.

"We'll leave you girls to talk," the elder Duncans said.

Susan's mother answered the phone on the second ring. Her hello sounded breathless and worried.

"Mom, it's me," Susan said.

"Thank heavens! Where are you? We've been worried sick since we noticed you and the gray were missing. Dad's out searching with a flashlight."

"I'm next door at the Duncans', the new neighbors. Star jumped the pasture fence and I went after him, but we're okay." Susan described Whitney's part and that she was going to walk the horse home along the road.

"No, wait there. Dad can come over and walk you back. The road's too narrow to be walking a horse alone in the dark. Were the Duncans upset?" Mrs. Holmes added quickly. Susan knew she was probably thinking of how the Wertheimers would have reacted to a horse loose on their property.

"Nope. You'll like them."

"Okay. Dad will be there in a few minutes."

51

Whitney had a feast laid out on the table when Susan turned from the desk. Not only was there a plate of chocolate-chip cookies, but a scrumptious-looking cake and a pan of fruit squares. Susan realized she was starving. She hadn't eaten much in the last few weeks. Suddenly she also realized that she hadn't felt so comfortable and happy since Dianna had left.

"My mother likes to bake," Whitney said when she saw Susan's expression. "Both my parents are professional cooks. That's how they got the restaurants started. I'm just glad I can eat anything I want and not gain an ounce."

"Me too." Susan happily dug into the piece of cake Whitney handed her.

"You haven't told me anything about yourself," Whitney said. "Do you have a real farm, or just horses?"

"It used to be a farm a long time ago, before we bought it. My parents run it as a riding stable now. We board and train horses and give lessons."

"Lucky you! Neither of my parents knows anything about horses, but I've been crazy about riding forever. I've been riding since I was six."

"You must be pretty good."

"Probably not as good as you, but I'm trying. What did you think of Bravo? I want to enter some shows with him, but we need more practice together."

"He's got nice conformation. What's his breeding?"

"Part Thoroughbred. That horse of yours looks like a Thoroughbred."

"He is," Susan agreed.

"Are there a lot of shows around here?"

"Tons," Susan answered through a mouthful of cake.

"At the Hunt Club, and some of the farms put on their own horse trials – you know what they are?"

Whitney nodded. "Like mini three-day events with dressage, cross country, and show jumping. I haven't ridden in anything like that, though. Have you?"

"Last year and the year before, I rode in novice and training classes on my Morgan mare, Jasmine. But I've outgrown her." Susan wondered as she spoke if she'd have the courage to ride in a horse trial again. Her smile faded a little.

But Whitney grinned as she polished off her fifth cookie and leaned back in the chair. "This is *exactly* what I dreamed of – having a place to ride and meeting someone to talk to about horses. And we'll even be in the same class. I've been helping my parents unpack, but tomorrow it's back to the grind for me."

"You're going to the regional school?" Susan asked in surprise.

"Sure. Where else would I go?"

"I just figured you'd be going to private school – Hotchkiss or something. Most of the rich kids around here do."

Whitney's dark eyes were twinkling. "You think we're rich? Boy, that's funny. My parents would love it."

Susan blushed. "Well, I mean, you can't be poor."

Whitney scowled thoughtfully. "No, we're not poor. But it's only in the last few years that the restaurants started doing really well." They were interrupted by a knock on the back door. Whitney jumped up. "Must be your father." She hurried to the door and opened it. "Hi, I'm Whitney. You must be Susan's father. Come on in."

"Hello, Whitney. Mitch Holmes. Thanks." He said as he stepped inside. "Nice to meet you, and sorry about all of this. I hope our horse didn't cause any problems."

"Nope." Whitney beamed. "It worked out just perfect. This is my mother and father," she added as her parents came back into the kitchen. "Mr. Holmes."

"Welcome to Norbridge," Mr. Holmes said as the adults shook hands. "I was hoping this place wouldn't be sold off to a developer after Mrs. Prendergast died."

"No, we'll be keeping it just the way it is."

"Are you horse people?"

Mr. Duncan laughed. "Far from it. I know the difference between the front and the back end of a horse, but that's about it. Our daughter's the horsewoman, though my wife and I want to get more involved now that we have this place."

"Stop by at our place any time if you need any pointers. We'd be glad to help you out."

"Thanks. We'll do that."

"Thank *you*, and your daughter," Mr. Holmes said. "Sorry again about the trouble."

"No problem."

Susan had risen and walked over to her father.

"The horse is out in the barn," Whitney said. "Come on, I'll show you."

Mr. Holmes waved good-bye to the Duncans. "I appreciate your giving Susan a hand."

"Any time," Mr. Duncan said. "I hope we'll be seeing a lot of her over here."

Evening Star nickered as Susan stepped into the stall and clipped on his shank. He nuzzled her shoulder as he followed her out. Mr. Holmes quickly and expertly looked the horse over. "He doesn't look any the worse for his adventure. Why did he jump out? Did you see? Something frighten him?"

"I don't know. I just looked up and saw him galloping toward the fence. He flew over." She didn't add that she wondered if Star was just miserable in his new home.

"Hmm." Mr. Holmes rubbed his chin. "Considering the height of the pasture fence, I'd say we might have a class jumper here after all." As they left the barn, Mr. Holmes flicked on his flashlight and thanked Whitney again.

"Yes, thanks," Susan added. "I'm glad I met you."

"See you at school tomorrow."

"Yup."

As Susan and her father headed back to the farm along the narrow country road, Mr. Holmes spoke quietly. "Everyone keeps telling me that this horse is a loner and doesn't trust anyone more than he has to. But I noticed the way he acted with you in the barn."

Susan had been thinking the same thing herself and wasn't sure how she felt about it.

"Maybe you ought to take over his grooming," her father said thoughtfully. "Some horses respond better when only one person is caring for them, and I'd like to see this guy do more than he's done so far."

Susan surprised herself with her answer. "I guess I could." Suddenly she found she did want to start grooming Evening Star, even if she wasn't willing to think beyond that. Had meeting Whitney something to do with her change of heart? She didn't know, but she knew she was glad they'd met, even if Whitney changed her mind about being Susan's friend after meeting the popular kids at school.

Evening Star softly nickered and touched Susan's shoulder with his nose. He seemed to be saying he liked the new arrangement too.

When Susan led Whitney to the school office on Monday morning, kids turned and stared. The stares weren't the kind that Susan usually got; they were wide-eyed and impressed. Whitney looked fabulous. Susan didn't understand exactly what it was that Whitney did to look so great – maybe it was the way she moved, and she had a real flare for clothes. Whitney didn't even seem to notice the attention she was getting, but Susan did. She wondered how anyone so tall could be so self-assured.

They ended up with the same homeroom, and since Susan already knew Whitney, the school secretary suggested that she show Whitney around for the first few days. Whitney was so friendly, she didn't need a lot of introductions. She just walked up to kids and started talking. By the end of Whitney's second day at school, *everybody* knew who she was. She was so sophisticated compared to most of the girls in the ninth-grade class. The girls were all awed to hear that she modeled in New York and impressed at how rich she must be if her parents had bought the old Prendergast estate. Tara was absolutely amazed when she saw Susan and Whitney sharing a lunch table and gabbing away like old friends. Susan smiled to herself.

But later in the week, in the girls' room, Susan overheard two of Tara's friends talking. "I can't believe it. Why would someone like Whitney Duncan want to be friends with Susan Holmes? It's so strange. Susan's such an absolute nothing. She always looks like such a mess. Her hair just sort of hangs there."

Susan froze in the stall, rigid with mortification. But they were right – she never looked in a mirror. She didn't much care what she wore as long as it covered her.

"I don't understand it at all," the second girl continued. "Tara's talked to Whitney. She's really neat – and her clothes! But it doesn't seem to bother her that she's hanging around with absolutely the wrong person."

"Oh, she'll figure it out. I mean, she's only been here a week."

The two girls left, but Susan stayed where she was, her hands clenched in fists. A week before she would have burst into tears to hear what she did, but suddenly she realized she was angry. Who did Tara and her friends think they were? All they cared about was the way a person looked. Susan knew that her friendship with Whitney was already deeper than that.

She didn't say anything to Whitney about what she'd heard, and Whitney acted exactly the same as the day they'd first met. Their friendship continued to grow. Whitney was engrossed in riding, and they could talk about horses for hours. One day at lunch, Whitney pulled a book about eventing from her backpack.

"Oh, I read that book," Susan said, recognizing the cover. "It's pretty good."

"I'm enjoying it," Whitney agreed. "But sometimes I don't understand some of the things they're talking about. There's no glossary." She put the book carefully to one side as she and Susan began eating their school lunches.

"What don't you understand?" Susan asked, taking a sip of milk.

"Well, they're talking about a cross-country course, and they mention different types of jumps. I can't tell what they are."

"You better learn," Susan said with a laugh. "You'll probably be going out on our cross-country course soon."

Whitney looked pleased at the unspoken invitation, then put down her sandwich and paged through the book.

"For example," she said, looking up at Susan quizzically, "what's the difference between a horizontal jump and a crossbar?"

"It's just like it sounds. A crossbar is two poles crossed over each other to make an X, and a horizontal jump is just one or more poles on top of each other. A parallel jump is two or more poles *next* to each other."

"Oh." Whitney nodded her understanding. "Okay. What's bullfinch?"

Susan took another sip of milk and wiped her lips. "It's a combination of a brush and either a two- or three-bar parallel."

"Uh huh. And what's a brush?" Whitney looked perplexed.

Susan laughed again. She had been using these terms practically her whole life; to her, they were like "shoe" or

59

"tree." It was an ego booster to realize that she could teach her sophisticated new friend something, and Whitney's enthusiasm was infectious.

"A brush looks like a thick hedge. Sometimes it's really a hedge and sometimes it's fake."

"I get it. And finally . . ." Whitney paused to pore through the book again. "What's a coop?"

"A coop is like a small half building; it's sort of supposed to look like a real chicken coop. That's why they call it that."

Whitney's brown eyes widened. "Great – I'm going to be jumping buildings."

Susan laughed. That was another thing she liked about Whitney – her sense of humor. Time and again Whitney had Susan giggling at her lightning-quick remarks. They thought alike about a lot of things, Susan realized – and they both knew what it was like to be very tall for their age, though Whitney handled it much better than Susan did. At the end of the week, Susan invited Whitney to come over to the farm after school.

Whitney accepted in a shot. "I've been dying to see your place. The only riding stables I've been to were in the city."

Susan took Whitney around the farm, introduced her to her mother, Kirin, and Joany, and showed her their twenty horses and their facilities. Furball, who tagged along during the tour, immediately approved of Whitney, rubbing against her legs and purring. Then Susan took Whitney for a walk around the cross-country course.

"Whoa," Whitney said when she saw some of the jumps on the course. "I don't think Bravo and I are ready for this yet."

60

"You can do it with enough practice," Susan assured her. "Bravo's got the height and build to handle a course like this – as long as he really loves to jump."

"Oh, he likes to jump, but I don't know about these."

"The jumps look bigger when you're on foot. They don't seem half as scary from the saddle."

"Have you jumped this course?"

"Some of it," Susan said, then felt that now familiar tightness in her stomach, wondering how she'd ever done it – wondering if she'd ever have the courage to do it again.

"When are we going to go riding together?" Whitney asked excitedly. "I don't want to try any of this stuff, but we've got plenty of riding trails at our place. Is your wrist strong enough for you to ride yet?"

"I shouldn't," Susan began, then bit her lip. She couldn't keep making excuses, and she especially didn't want to make excuses to Whitney. She needed to talk to someone – to finally get it all off her chest. Whitney definitely seemed like the person to tell.

"No, that's not the whole truth," Susan admitted. "The truth is, I've been afraid . . . it was an awful fall . . . and it was my own fault." In a rush of words, she told Whitney what had happened, how she'd wanted to show Tara up and had jumped a green horse, how humiliated she'd been, and how terrified she was now to get back in the saddle. "So I've been pretending my wrist still hurts and my ribs are still sore. I don't want them all to know how scared I am," she finished lamely.

"Hey, listen, I know how you feel. I fell once and broke my collarbone. I nearly didn't ride again, but I had an instructor who just kept after me – wouldn't give me a break. Once I got in the saddle again, I was okay. I mean, it took a little while for me to relax, but pretty soon I was fine. And boy, am I glad now she made me do it!"

"It's not just getting hurt," Susan confessed. "Riding's the only thing I've ever been good at. You've seen I'm not popular at school or anything. But I was really proud of my riding. I was happy and felt good when I was riding. It made up for all the other stuff. And then I totally lose control in front of my class, including Tara Pendleton – mess up completely! A week later Tara's riding the same horse and taking him over the same jumps perfectly –"

"Oh, I heard all about it and how good Tara is – from Tara." Whitney made a face.

"She told you about my accident?" Susan cried.

"So?" Whitney shrugged. "I hate people who have to brag all the time and put other people down doing it. I knew someone like her at my old school. She was a jerk."

Susan could only stare. She'd never, ever heard anyone put Tara down. She couldn't believe Whitney was doing it now. "But she's the most popular girl in our class – she always has been. Everybody wants to be friends with her."

"I don't."

"You don't?"

"Nope. I've got better things to do. And you shouldn't listen to anything she says either. I'll bet you're a better rider now than she'll ever be. Besides, who wants to be one of Tara's crowd anyway? I like you better because you're different. Hey, let's go visit Evening Star. I brought some carrots. He's really a super looking horse. You could do some fantastic stuff with him . . . and you wouldn't have to start jumping right away. You could build up your confidence again little by little."

Susan looked over at her new friend, shook her head in bemusement, then smiled. *Wow*, she thought. Was she ever glad that Whitney had moved next door!

That night, when Susan climbed into bed and turned off her light, she thought a lot about what Whitney had said. It was absolutely incredible that Whitney didn't care about Tara's opinions. It was pretty great. Just thinking about it made Susan smile. Thinking about riding again was another thing. Deep inside she wanted to – badly. She could picture herself in the saddle on Star's back. The nightmare memory of her fall hadn't gone away, but Whitney's words stayed in her mind.

Over the next week Susan noticed a change in herself. She didn't feel quite so out of it at school. After all, Whitney was as tall as she was, and her height didn't bother her. Susan felt happier at home, too, now that she'd started grooming Star and taking him for walks around the yard. Her parents weren't about to put him out in the pasture again after he'd leaped the fence, but he needed daily exercise. Susan admitted to herself now that she'd always been drawn to him and that maybe she'd been stupid to try to keep her distance. Star certainly seemed to want her nearby, brushing his silky gray coat or just hanging around his stall talking. His new contentment at having someone who cared was obvious. He pricked his ears at the sound of Susan's voice and seemed to listen as she talked about Whitney and School. "It's really funny," she told him thoughtfully. "The kids are starting to act different. They don't ignore me like they used to. A couple of girls in my

English class actually asked me to go to the football game with them after school. Was I shocked or what? Of course, they asked Whitney to go too. I couldn't because I have stuff to do around here in the afternoon, but was I ever amazed."

Star craned his head around and whuffed her cheek.

Susan grinned. "I don't even feel sick to my stomach in the mornings when I go to catch the bus." She paused and frowned. "I know I'll never be popular. I think kids are treating me differently because Whitney's my friend. I still haven't figured out why she *wants* to be my friend . . . but it's okay."

Star gave a soft snort and looked at her. Then he stepped away from his hay net and pushed his nose against her shoulder. She reached up and rubbed his ears and laid her forehead against his cheek.

"I wish he'd show that kind of trust in me." Susan lifted her head and looked over to see Kirin standing there with her arms folded on the top of the stall door.

"It's incredible the way he is with you," Kirin continued. "You're getting through to him. I tried him out the other day in the ring and got zero response from him, no matter what I did. It's like he's waiting for his rider to pull a fast one. Your mother said the same thing when she rode him. *You* ought to take him out."

Susan swallowed. Maybe Whitney understood Susan's fears, but Susan doubted Kirin would. She'd seen Kirin take some pretty bad falls while she was training Charming on the cross-country course, and it had never fazed her. She'd gotten right back in the saddle.

"Oh, I forgot about your wrist," Kirin said, saving her.

64

"But I'm beginning to see why Maxine got rid of him. Nice animal, but he just doesn't put his heart into it."

Was it possible, Susan wondered, that Maxine had killed Star's desire to do well? She hadn't seriously thought of that before, and it was a pretty awful prospect. Her mother and Kirin were incredible riders, and if they couldn't succeed . . .

Susan shook the thought away. She patted the big gray's neck. "You're going to do fine, aren't you, boy?"

That Sunday morning Tara pranced around the stable, bragging about her first-place finish on Jocko at the Hunt Club show the day before. Susan had heard all about it from Joany, who'd gone with several of the farm's students. As she was filling hay nets, Susan overheard Tara talking to one of the boarders. "I've decided to buy my own horse," Tara trilled. "Jocko's a nice animal, but I can't go much further on him."

"What kind of horse are you thinking about?" the boarder asked.

"Oh, a Thoroughbred. They're so consistent."

Susan snorted at Tara's choice of words – like Tara knew what she was talking about.

"Have you picked one out yet?"

"Maybe," Tara answered mysteriously.

Susan shrugged. What did she care if Tara bought a horse or not? Tara would be just as unbearable.

Later that morning, before Lyle headed back to the University of Connecticut, he decided to take Star out to the schooling ring. He hadn't ridden the big gray yet and was curious. Susan watched a little anxiously from the end of the stable building. She'd been at school when her mother and Kirin had worked Star, and she needed to see for herself what they were talking about – and if Lyle's riding would make a difference. Maybe after Maxine, Star just didn't like female riders.

Lyle worked Star at a trot around the ring, then put him through some basic schooling figures – figure eights and serpentines – snakelike curves down the length of the ring. Star obeyed, but he looked ready to shy at the slightest disturbance, and his movements were tense and stiff. His strides had none of the graceful fluidity Susan had noticed when he was out in the pasture or on the first day she'd seen him, before Maxine had forced him over that water jump. He wasn't relaxing at all. He wasn't working with his rider.

Susan saw her brother frown and try to extend Star's stride. "Come on, loosen up," she heard him mutter, putting Star into a canter. Susan shook her head. Star wasn't extending himself at all as Lyle worked him left around the ring. And it was even worse when they circled right. The horse looked like he was tripping all over himself and had absolutely no suppleness going around the turns. Susan shook her head in puzzled confusion. This wasn't the horse she knew at all!

Lyle looked fed up when he finally rode Star out of the ring. Star didn't look any happier as they approached the stable, but as soon as the horse saw Susan, he pricked his ears and whickered.

"Well, at least he likes somebody around here," Lyle grouched.

Susan automatically held Star's head and rubbed his nose as Lyle dismounted. "He wasn't putting out at all, was he?" she said unhappily.

"I might as well have been sitting on a mechanical stuffed animal. Mom and Kirin are right. He does what you ask him, but he's uptight. You know he's only doing it because he has to, not because he wants to."

"He's weak on his right side. He needs to build up those muscles." Susan said.

"No kidding! He was practically falling over his own feet." Lyle sounded frustrated. "I thought you were supposed to be taking care of him. Why haven't you had him out?"

"Mom and Kirin ride him while I'm at school . . . and I only just took him over."

"What's the matter with you?" Lyle barked. "He's been here for over a month. He could be a perfect mount for you if you'd put some time into him! And don't give me that garbage about your wrist not being healed. It's healed enough to do a little schooling. I hear you haven't been teaching any classes, either."

Susan's face was beet red. Lyle didn't understand, but before she could stumble out an explanation, he handed her Star's reins. "I've got too much to do to waste time with him. I'm taking Sir George out." Without a backward glance he stalked off.

Lyle's words ate at her. He knew she was making excuses. What *was* the matter with her? Why couldn't she get up the courage even to try? She had to do something soon. Her parents had started giving her funny, questioning looks, and she knew it wouldn't be long before they started pushing her.

She thought it all through as she walked Star to cool him out before putting him back in his stall. The leaves had fallen, but they were having a few days of Indian summer and it was beautiful out in the back meadows.

Star seemed to enjoy it too. His head was up and his ears pricked as they walked. There seemed to be an extra bounce in his stride. Why couldn't he show that in the schooling ring?

"What are we going to do with you?" Susan asked the horse. "Or me? We're a real team. You won't show them what you can do, and I'm afraid to ride again. Maybe you're afraid too – that someone will ask too much of you too soon, like Maxine did."

Star eyed Susan, then playfully gave her a nudge with his nose.

"Would it make a difference if I rode you?" The horse whickered, but obviously he hadn't understood her words. "I don't know what to do. Just give me a little more time."

That night at dinner Susan found out she didn't have any more time. "Tara Pendleton asked if Evening Star was for sale," her father told her.

Susan nearly dropped her fork, staring at him. "Tara?" she gasped.

"No one's having much luck retraining him, and Tara wants to give it a shot. I told her he needed a lot of work and might not be a good investment, but she said she's seen you walking him and she fell in love with him. She's been riding very well. If she buys him, it'll mean he'll stay here as a new boarder, but I don't know if I'm ready to sell him yet. I'd like to give him a little more time, to see if we can do anything with him ourselves. I told her I'd let her know in two weeks." He glanced over at Susan.

Susan's throat was so tight, she couldn't get any words

68

out. Her thoughts raced. Tara wanted to buy Star? She had to tell her parents that she wanted him herself. But what if she kept him and still couldn't get up the courage to ride? To do Star justice, she'd have to do more than ride him in the schooling ring; she'd have to jump him. Her stomach immediately clenched. But she couldn't let Tara have him!

She barely heard a word her parents said for the rest of the meal. All she could think about was Tara sitting in Star's saddle, gloating. As soon as she'd cleared the table, Susan slipped out of the cozy kitchen and went out to the barn. She had made up her mind what she was going to do. Her knees shook at the thought, but it was now or never.

"Easy, boy," Susan said a few minutes later as she took Star out of his stall and put him in cross ties. The cross ties led from each side of his bridle and held Star in place in the stable aisle. The horse knew something strange was going on and fidgeted, dancing from hoof to hoof, flicking his ears and snorting softly. He was never taken out of his stall at night.

"Shh," Susan told him. "We've got to be quiet. This is our secret. We're going to go for a little ride – just you and me."

She slid the saddle she'd brought from the tack room onto his back and tightened the girth. Then she put on his bridle. Her stomach was flip-flopping crazily.

Furball watched from his perch on the stall door. His wise yellow eyes seemed to glint their approval.

"Okay, Star," Susan soothed as she unclipped the cross ties and took his reins. "We're going to go to the indoor ring and just do a little simple stuff. This is going to be a test for me, but I've got to do it. I can't let Tara Pendleton have you."

Susan led him down the barn aisle, through the open door, and into the rear yard. At seven it was already dark, but the outside barn lights lit their way as she led him down the short path to the huge enclosed rectangle of the indoor ring. Everyone had left for the night, and her parents couldn't see the indoor ring from the house. She felt safe as she unbarred the door, reached around to flick on the overhead lights, and walked Star inside.

Immediately he lifted his head and looked around, flaring his delicate nostrils. He hadn't been in the ring before. Susan made soothing noises as she refastened the door and led him out over the cushiony wood-chip surface toward the center of the ring. A few jump posts, rails and barrels were clustered at one end, but the ring wouldn't be used regularly until the weather turned cold.

Susan pulled down the stirrup irons, threw the reins over Star's head, and went to his left side. Her legs were like water, and she felt suddenly dizzy. *I can't do it*, she thought. *I can't. I'm too nervous. He'll know. He'll bolt with me.*

Star craned his head around curiously and gave her a soft look from one huge brown eye. He blew out a sweet-scented breath and stood patiently, waiting. It was unusual for a highly bred, excitable Thoroughbred like Evening Star to show such patience. It was as if the horse sensed her anxiety and was encouraging her.

Susan swallowed and took several slow, deep breaths. "Susan Holmes, you are going to do this," she told herself firmly. "You're going to prove that you can."

She placed her left hand, holding the reins, at the base of Star's neck, slid her left foot into the stirrup iron, hopped, and swung her right leg over the saddle, quickly inserting her foot in the right stirrup. Her heart was pounding, but she was in the saddle!

One down, she thought. Star stood, still patient, as she automatically settled herself, made sure the girth was tight enough, and gathered a rein in each hand. Her right wrist was still wrapped in an Ace bandage, but it didn't interfere with the use of her hand. Then she looked up between Star's ears.

"Okay, now what?" She sighed shakily. "Let's walk, Star." She tightened her legs slightly, and Star moved forward smoothly toward the perimeter of the oval ring. Susan tightened her left rein and walked him counterclockwise. Star moved easily along, but Susan was as tense as a coiled spring. Her brain felt numb; she couldn't think ahead. She could think only about the present moment and getting through it.

Twice they walked around the oval under the bright lights. It was all so familiar to Susan – the horsey scent of the ring, the motion of the horse, the feel of the reins, the position of her legs and feet, the sound of Star's hoofs as they hit the soft ground. She had done this so many times before. Unconsciously she began to relax a little.

Turning Star, she walked him the other way. His ears flicked back toward her as if he was waiting – wondering what this was all about. "Good boy," she praised softly, though her voice was wavery. She knew, even as she spoke, that walking the big gray wasn't much of a test at all – for either of them. But it was the more complicated things that frightened her.

Finally, as they came down one side of the ring, she steeled her courage, took another deep and steadying breath, clucked to Star, and tightened her legs. "Let's trot."

He snorted softly, then sprang forward at the brisker

72

pace. Again they circled the ring, with Susan posting in the saddle, lifting her weight as he lifted his outside shoulder. At first she knew her movements were stiff and tense, but Star was moving beautifully and comfortably. They'd circled the ring several times before Susan relaxed enough to realize there was a spring in Star's step that hadn't been there when Lyle had ridden him. She was sure it wasn't her imagination. Star actually seemed to be enjoying himself!

To test him and her impressions, she started him through a figure eight, turning him toward the center of the ring as they completed the top loop. As they crossed the center, she sat a beat in the saddle and rose on the opposite shoulder, circling him through the second loop. He responded instantly to her pressure on the rein, although she did notice he didn't seem quite as comfortable working to the right.

She completed three more figures, concentrating on his movement and forgetting her own fears in the excitement of knowing the horse was trying for her. He seemed like a different animal than the one Lyle had ridden! His strides were full of energy and spring. Could it be possible that Star really was putting out that little bit extra for her? "Unbelievable," she whispered.

Star heard, and his ears flicked back. He gave a little toss of his head in acknowledgment.

Susan was so engrossed in the seeming change in Star that she didn't even think about what she was doing as she put him into a canter. All her ingrained knowledge came to hand as she gave him the signals – she didn't have to think. At a touch of her rein and heel, he instantly changed gaits, leading out with his left foreleg as she moved him counterclockwise around the perimeter of the ring.

Perfect, Susan thought as she sat back to the rocking-horse motion of the canter. Star was moving with ease – relaxing, cantering, effortlessly.

Elated, totally forgetting herself, she slowed him, turned, and cantered him to the right. Susan immediately felt a problem. For a second she thought he was on the wrong lead. He felt off balance. She glanced down and saw he was leading out with his right foreleg, just as he should. But he now felt almost as awkward as he'd looked when Lyle had ridden him. When they came around the end of the ring, he felt stiff bending into the right turn. Star was obviously trying his best, but he was uncomfortable. There was no point in pushing him. Susan slowed him down to a trot and guided him through a few of the figure eights that he'd done so well. All the while she was thinking. Could the weakness on his right side have something to do with his having been initially trained as a racehorse?

She could remember reading an article in one of her riding magazines about the special reschooling racers needed. Races were always run counterclockwise around the track, and horses in training were galloped only counterclockwise. They tended to be left sided – the muscles on their left sides were stronger than the muscles on their right. They also were less flexible bending right. She'd have to dig the article out, but it made sense. She slowed Star to a walk and patted his neck. "That's it, big guy!" Susan said excitedly. "That has to be it!"

Star craned his head around and looked at her as if he knew he hadn't done well.

"Oh, it's not your fault, Star. You've never had a chance to strengthen the muscles on your right. We're going to have to take you right back to the beginning and do a lot of work on the longe line, strengthen up those muscles."

Maxine should have done all that, Susan thought. How could a decent horsewoman ask a horse to jump a course where he'd be turning tightly both right and left without giving him the preliminary schooling? Maxine must have noticed his weakness. Was she just too impatient to take the time? Susan wondered too why her mother and Kirin hadn't noticed either. But Star had been performing so badly overall for them, they might have missed the dramatic difference in his canter on the right lead.

Star nickered, and Susan leaned forward to hug his neck. "It's okay, boy. We're going to fix those weak muscles. Tomorrow afternoon, I'll start working you on the longe. Before you know it, you'll be in perfect shape. You've showed me you can put your heart into it!"

She walked Star around for a few more minutes to cool him out, then dismounted and led him out of the ring. After turning off the lights and shutting the door, she took him back to the barn. All was still quiet. Their secret was safe. In the barn she untacked Star and settled him in his stall. Then she threw her arms around his neck and gave him a kiss. He nickered and gently lipped her sleeve. "Good night, buddy." She sighed. "And thank you!"

Only as she fastened the stall door and bent to pick up his saddle and bridle did her feat completely sink in, "I did it!" she gasped. "I rode again! I can do it!"

Star looked over the stall door and bobbed his head. Furball came trotting down the aisle, rubbed his fat body against Susan's boots, then jumped nimbly onto the stall door. He slowly blinked his yellow eyes at her. His face wore that catlike look of satisfaction. Susan laughed and blew both him and Star a kiss, then headed for the tack room.

She was walking on air as she went back to the house and into the kitchen. Her mother called to her from the den. "Is your homework done, Susan? It's after eight."

"I'm going to finish it now. Good night."

"Good night," both her parents called. They sounded perfectly normal. They didn't suspect what she'd been doing for the past hour. Susan poured a glass of milk and grabbed a handful of cookies, then jogged up the back stairs to her bedroom. She set the milk and cookies on her desk, reached for the phone, and dialed Whitney's number.

"Whitney, I did it!" she cried as soon as Whitney picked up.

There was a second's silence, then Whitney answered excitedly, "You mean you rode again?"

"Yeah! I took Star to the indoor ring tonight. Nobody knows, so don't say anything yet. I want to be sure we're both doing okay before I tell anyone. And guess what else happened. My parents told me tonight that Tara wants to buy Star!"

"What?" Whitney yelped. "You're not going to let her, are you?"

"No way! There's *no way* I'm going to let her get near him. She'd be as bad as Maxine, even if she and Jocko did manage to get a first at that show last weekend."

"Yeah, and she's not letting anyone forget it. Have your parents already told her she could have him?"

"Not yet. My father told her he won't decide for a couple of weeks – that Star needs a lot of work and may never turn into anything. But after tonight, I know that's

76

not true. You should have seen him! He's weak on his right side, but he was really trying. He was altogether different from when Lyle rode him." Happily Susan told Whitney every detail.

"See, I told you! I knew that horse was perfect for you. I can't wait until the two of us go riding. You can bring him over here to practice. You'll show Tara."

Susan smiled. Suddenly she knew that she would.

For the rest of the week, Susan spent most of every afternoon working Star on the longe in the indoor ring. The mild weather had held out, so classes were still outside. Susan always waited until the rest of the staff were busy before taking Star out. Since she'd been taking him out for walks anyway, no one paid much attention to them as Susan led Star behind the indoor ring and entered through the rear door. They were able to work in privacy, although she knew that wouldn't last long. It was getting darker earlier, and soon the temperatures would drop and classes would be moving inside. She'd have to find another time to school him.

He was alert and eager as she worked him on the longe, circling him around her at the end of the long line, first at a walk, then a trot, and then a canter. She concentrated on his weak, right side, working him primarily in a clockwise direction. When he looked like he was tiring, she stopped and worked him to the left, letting him finish off his lesson strongly. Finishing on a positive note helped Star's morale and encouraged him to keep trying.

Susan realized how much she'd missed working with the horses during her self-imposed exile. She began to realize

77

too just how sore and aching she'd been inside. "But that's over," she told Star as she fed him a carrot after his lesson. "At least the worst part is over. I'm riding again, and I've got you, though I'm still afraid of jumping." She sighed. "It's silly, isn't it? I've ridden all my life, and I know you'd never deliberately hurt me, but just thinking about it makes me sick to my stomach."

Star crunched his carrot as she talked, giving her a long, soft look. "Yeah, I know. I'm going to be all right – someday. The main thing is that you're doing great. Tara isn't going to get you now."

Whitney came home with Susan on Friday. She'd been begging Susan to let her see Star's progress, and after a week Susan felt like they were ready. With Whitney standing guard, Susan smuggled Star's tack out of the tack room. That day she was going to ride him over cavalletti. Quickly she tacked up Star in his stall and threw a sheet over him. Anyone looking closely would notice the saddle underneath, but they wouldn't see it from a distance. The girls took Star down to the indoor ring, Whitney giggling at the secrecy.

Once they were inside, Susan removed the sheet and worked Star on the longe under tack. Whitney watched with concentration as Susan circled Star around her at different paces.

"I'm glad I'm getting to see this," Whitney said. "I've never known enough about it, and you sure know what you're doing."

Susan hadn't thought about it, but she guessed she did know what she was doing. She'd been helping to train horses for so long, she just took it for granted.

"Come and hold him for a second," she asked when she felt Star had been warmed up and limbered. "I want to set up a cavalletti." While Whitney held the horse, Susan collected half a dozen poles and laid them flat out on the ground about four feet apart. The object was to ride a horse through and teach him to lift his feet over the poles and adjust his stride accordingly.

When she was satisfied, Susan walked back to Whitney and Star. "Okay, boy, I'm pretty sure you've done this before, but let's give it a try." She pulled down the stirrups, then lifted the reins over his head. She took a deep breath, realizing she was nervous. She hadn't ridden him since her first try, and now Whitney was watching. But she swallowed, put her left foot in the stirrup, and mounted.

Star flicked his ears in excitement. Susan guessed that he had been getting bored with the longe line and was looking forward to something new. Susan checked the girth, gathered the reins, and settled herself. She turned Star toward the top of the ring, then turned him again so that he was facing the cavalletti. She'd walk him through first, to familiarize him with what was expected, then take him through at a trot.

Star eyed the obstacles on the ground and lifted his feet over them carefully as they walked through. He understood what was expected, and when Susan brought him around and trotted him through, he came through cleanly, lifting his legs high.

Susan laughed, feeling her own nervousness drain away. "I didn't think he'd go through so clean the first time!"

They went through several more times, approaching the

obstacle from both directions. Then Susan had Whitney move the poles just slightly farther apart.

"I want to extend his stride," she explained.

Again Star went through nicely, but he misjudged the last pole and ticked it with his hoof. "That's okay, boy," Susan told him. "These are a little farther apart. Let's try it again."

After one more perfect pass, Susan called it quits on a good note. She was thrilled at how quickly Star was learning and how hard he was trying. But she couldn't help wondering why he was doing this for her when he'd behaved so unwillingly for everyone else. Was it because they'd made a mental connection? Sometimes Susan was sure Star could read her mind – that he knew how much she'd hated the way Maxine had treated him. Animals did have a sixth sense. They knew who their friends were; they knew whom they could trust. Star seemed instinctively to understand that Susan was working for him, too.

Smiling, she turned to ride back to Whitney. In a few days she'd feel confident enough to tell her family and the staff what she'd accomplished. But as she turned, she clanked over toward the doorway and froze. Her brother was standing there. He must have just arrived home for the weekend.

Lyle grinned and flashed her a thumbs-up. "Good going," he called, then made a quick exit from the barn.

"Oh no," Susan groaned as she reached Whitney's side and dismounted. "It'll be all over the stable in two seconds. Lyle will definitely tell everyone I'm out here riding Star."

"What's wrong with that?" Whitney asked. "Maybe it's time you let everyone know, especially if Tara wants to buy Star. You've only got another week."

"I wanted to feel really sure of myself before everyone found out. I don't want a bunch of people coming by watching and making comments. I'll be a wreck all over again."

"They aren't going to be bad comments."

Susan sighed. "I guess I just wanted to do this all by myself . . . I don't feel very sure of myself yet."

"I can understand that," Whitney agreed, "but it's too late now."

Yet no one said anything when Susan, Whitney, and Star went back to the barn. Whitney had already smuggled Star's saddle and bridle back to the tack room, and Susan was grooming him, when Kirin stopped by the stall.

"Hi, Susan. How are you doing, Whitney?" Kirin asked. "I thought you were going to bring your horse over here for some practice on the jumps."

"I am," Whitney told her. "Any time now."

"Good. You thinking about entering any shows in the spring?"

"I hope to."

"You'll like the circuit here. Well, I'd better go. I've got some paperwork to do in the office. By the way, he's looking good, Susan. I don't know what you're doing, but you've got the right touch." Kirin strode up the barn aisle, and Susan and Whitney exchanged glances.

"Looks like your brother didn't say anything."

"Hmm," Susan murmured. "I'm surprised."

Whitney's mother picked her up just before dinner. Susan had wanted her to stay for dinner and spend the night, but Whitney's parents had company coming.

"Boring!" Whitney said to Susan as she was leaving. "But I'll see you tomorrow."

As Susan walked back to the house, she met her brother taking his horse back to the barn. She couldn't avoid him.

"So, Brat, you finally got in his saddle," he said bluntly, but he was smiling.

"Who did you tell?" Susan immediately asked.

Her brother's grin widened. "I thought you looked kind of sneaky down there. What's up? Why all the secrecy?"

"Oh, nothing . . . I've just been working him on my own." But Susan couldn't meet her brother's eye.

"It's a good thing you finally are. I hear one of the students is interested in buying him."

Susan looked up.

"I mentioned to Dad that maybe he ought to hold off selling the horse for a while." Lyle's blue eyes were twinkling. "Don't worry, I didn't tell him why I thought so. If you want to keep his training a big secret, that's your business. It doesn't make any sense to me," he said with a shrug. "But while he keeps coming along like he seems to be, I'll buy it."

Susan gave her brother a relieved smile. "Thanks."

"I wouldn't keep his progress a secret too much longer, though," Lyle added.

Her brother's warning stayed in her mind, and late the next morning she understood why. Susan had just put the school horses that weren't being ridden out in the pasture and was returning to the barn. She stepped into the dim interior when she heard Tara's voice carrying from the stable office. Susan stopped and slid into one of the empty stalls to listen.

"Jocko went pretty well today," Tara was saying.

Joany's voice answered. "I thought you had a great lesson."

"But I don't think I'm advancing as fast as I should on Jocko." Tara complained. "I need a better horse, with decent breeding. Jocko just doesn't have what it takes. That's the horse I'm buying – Evening Star."

"Oh yeah?" Joany said. Susan could imagine the instructor's raised brows. Tara sounded so sure of herself. "He's a nice looking animal," Joany added, "but he's got some problems. He won't be easy to train."

"I could handle him. Didn't I turn Jocko around after Susan lost control of him?"

"That was just a freak accident. The horse got over-excited that day."

Thank you, Joany, Susan thought.

"Besides," Joany continued, "you won't have any trouble controlling Evening Star. The problem is getting him to put out. He's got an attitude when a rider gets on his back. He doesn't want to perform."

"He just needs firm handling and to learn he can't get away with it," Tara said confidently.

Susan knew Joany wouldn't agree with that. But she also knew Joany wouldn't get in an argument with a student – especially one who paid for as many hours as Tara did.

"I don't know if the Holmeses want to sell him," Joany said mildly. "I think they're looking at him to be Susan's new mount."

"What a waste that would be," Tara snipped. "Besides, I've already talked to them."

"Susan's the only one who's gotten close to him –"

Tara cut Joany short. "She hasn't even *ridden* since she fell, and I could do a better job with him. They'll sell him to me. My father's willing to pay a lot more than the Holmeses paid for him. Then I'll put him right into training for the spring shows – get him jumping, like he should be."

That comment alone showed how little Tara really knew about training. "We won't be selling Evening Star to you, Tara Pendleton," Susan said under her breath. "Not if I have anything to do with it!" But now she knew she had to tell her parents.

Susan was standing at her locker when Tara passed with her clique of friends. Susan had her back to Tara, but she knew Tara was deliberately talking loudly enough so that Susan could overhear.

"This horse I'm buying is incredible," Tara was saying. "Wait till you see what I do with him in the spring. He's going to need a lot of work, of course . . . Susan just hasn't done anything with him . . ."

Whitney walked up to Susan's locker just as Tara had passed, and snorted. "Listen to her! Someone ought to gag her."

Susan chuckled. "She won't be so happy when she finds out she's not getting Star."

"You talked to your parents?"

"Well, sort of. I was going to, but last night at dinner they said they'd decided not to sell Star after all. I have a feeling they know I've been training him, but I don't know how, unless Lyle blabbed. I think Kirin knows too. She came up to Star's stall when I was grooming him yesterday and gave me this big wink – like she knew all about my secret."

"So your brother did tell everyone."

"No. From the way Kirin was smiling, I think she's known for a while – and I thought I was being so sneaky!" Susan grinned.

"I guess you don't have to be sneaky anymore."

"Well, I haven't ridden him outside the ring yet." Susan chewed her lip. "That'll be a whole new test. I don't know how he'll react. Maybe it'll remind him of the way Maxine treated him on the cross-country course."

"What are you doing this afternoon?" Whitney said suddenly.

Susan frowned. "Nothing except what I usually do."

"It's a nice day. Bring Star over to my house. We'll take him and Bravo for a trail ride. If we do it right after school, we can get in a good ride before dark. You know I've been dying to, and there won't be anyone around except me, so you won't get all uptight."

Susan considered for the briefest moment, then nodded. "All right! Let's do it!"

Whitney grinned. "I'll get off the bus at your stop," she offered. "That way we can walk Star over to my house together. Tara doesn't have a lesson today, does she?"

"No, but she's been finding excuses to come by the stable almost every day."

"Why are we worrying about her, anyway? You can go anywhere you want with your own horse."

Everything went perfectly. No one was around to see Susan taking Star's saddle and bridle from the tack room; they all had things to do. Susan and Whitney led a tacked Star down the drive with no one the wiser.

After they'd reached the Duncans' and Whitney had tacked up Bravo, the girls set out across the meadow behind the barn. The air was crisp, but the November sky was cloudless and the slanting rays of sunlight were warm. Bundled in heavy sweaters, the girls didn't feel chilled at all. And the horses loved the cool, tangy air.

The girls trotted the horses down one of the wide pathways under the now bare-branched trees. Susan had felt a slight twinge of nervousness as they'd set out – she really didn't know how Star would behave in open country. After the way Maxine had treated him, he couldn't have good memories. But he was wonderful – alert, but quick to listen to her every signal. They hadn't gone far before Susan began to relax and enjoy herself.

"See," Whitney said. "All you needed to do was get in the saddle one more time. You're so natural, once you stopped being afraid. You ride like you've done it forever."

"Well." Susan blushed. "I guess I have . . . since I was three, anyway." It felt great to hear Whitney's compliment.

"Now we can really start planning for the spring shows," Whitney added, her eyes bright. "We can train together! It's going to be fantastic!"

Susan hadn't thought that far ahead. She hadn't even jumped Star yet, and she still had deep fears. But Whitney's enthusiasm was contagious. Susan smiled back widely.

They ended their ride with a rousing canter back across the meadow. Both the Duncans were watching from the drive as the girls rode up. "It's great to see you two out riding," Mr. Duncan said. "Looks like you had a good time."

Susan nodded. Her cheeks were rosy and her eyes bright.

"The best." Whitney grinned. "I finally got her over here. We'll be doing a lot of riding now."

"It's a good thing you got out today. The weather forecast is for freezing rain and cold. Winter's here."

Whitney glanced at Susan. "Looks like you won't have the indoor ring to yourself anymore."

Susan rubbed her hand over Star's sleek neck. "No more secrets now."

Susan felt so good that she decided to ride Star back along the road, rather than lead him. She talked quietly to him as they walked on the shoulder of the road. The grass was still green, but it wouldn't be for much longer. "You were great today, boy," she told him. "It feels so good to be riding again, and I don't know if I would have done it this soon if it weren't for you." Star flicked back his ears, listening. "And it's only going to get better from here."

As Susan rode up the drive toward the stable, one of Joany's beginner classes was just breaking up. The students were leading their horses from the ring. Joany had followed her class on foot. She looked startled to see Susan up on the big gray, but she quickly gave Susan a nod and big grin.

Unfortunately, Tara was standing outside the stable office talking to two young riders who boarded their horses at the farm. She took one look at Susan and Star, and her blue eyes popped wide in amazement. Just as quickly, her mouth tightened and she glared at them. She strode up to Susan angrily.

"What are you doing riding Star?" she demanded. "I'm buying him, and I don't want him ruined!"

For an instant Susan flinched. It was an automatic reaction, the way she always behaved around Tara. Then something snapped inside her. She straightened her shoulders and stared down. "You won't be buying him, Tara."

"Oh yes I will." Tara smiled confidently.

"Wrong. Evening Star is mine. I'll be riding him."

Two angry red spots blossomed on Tara's cheeks. She stood with fists clenched, eyes blazing in fury as Susan's words sank in. "You're doing this on purpose . . ." She finally sputtered, ". . . just so I can't have him! But you'll never do as much with him as I could –"

"You're wrong!" Susan glared back.

"Well, don't expect another offer from me – not after you've ruined him!"

"He's not for sale, Tara. Especially to you." Susan tapped Star with her heels and started trotting off. As she did, she saw Kirin standing in the office doorway. She was grinning, and she gave Susan a big wink.

Susan felt a heady rush of happiness as she walked Star into the barn. She reached up and hugged Star's neck. "I did it," she cried with her cheek pressed against his neck. "I finally stood up to Tara. I don't know how I ever let her get to me like I did, but not anymore. And it's all because of you. And Whitney, of course."

Star craned his head around and gently nuzzled her shoulder.

"We're going to go places from now on," she said with a sigh.

The next few weeks were the happiest Susan had had in a long time – since before Dianna left. Most of her happiness was due to Star and the fact that she was riding again. Her confidence was returning, and the horse was improving by leaps and bounds. The longeing had strengthened his muscles, and he was working just as easily now to the right as to the left. And because he was feeling stronger with proper training, he was more confident, too. Soon he'd be ready to start jumping raised cavalletti, although the thought of jumping still left Susan feeling weak-kneed. She decided she wouldn't think about jumping until the actual time came to do it.

Whitney and Susan were spending more and more time together. Whitney brought Bravo over to the farm several days a week, and the girls worked their horses together in the indoor ring when no classes were in session. Sometimes Joany, Kirin, or Susan's parents stopped by to watch for a few minutes, but they all seemed to understand that Susan wanted and needed to do Star's reschooling herself.

The only one around the stable who definitely was not happy was Tara. She glowered whenever she saw Susan, and at school she still had plenty of nasty comments. "She always rides when no one's around," Susan overheard Tara tell one of her friends. "She's probably too embarrassed to let anyone see."

Susan did her best to ignore Tara, and surprisingly, she could, now that she'd finally stood up for herself. But Tara was still at the stable as much as ever. She'd found another horse to buy and was constantly talking about his bloodline and how much her father had paid for him.

"Does she think she's going to ride better because her father paid a fortune for her horse?" Whitney said with a laugh one cold afternoon when the girls were sitting in Whitney's big bedroom.

90

"But she's been riding okay," Susan said. "I watched her from the office window the other day."

Whitney wrinkled her nose. "Too bad. What am I saying? She still won't stand a chance against the two of us in the spring horse trials."

"I hope," Susan answered. She didn't feel as confident as Whitney. If she was ever going to enter any horse trials, she'd have to start training Star over jumps, and it was already December.

Whitney suddenly walked over to the closets that covered one wall of the room, opened the folding doors, and started rummaging through the hangers. Susan stared from her spot on the bed. She'd never seen so many clothes except in a store. Every so often Whitney would yank something off a hanger and fling it over a nearby chair.

"What are you doing?" Susan asked.

"I was thinking when I got dressed this morning that I don't need all this stuff. I don't wear half of it, and I can't find what I want because the closet's so packed."

"Where did you get all those clothes? I mean, if you don't like them, why did you buy them?"

"Some of it's from modeling assignments, and I get freebies all the time from designers. They figure they'll get advertising if I wear their stuff."

The pile on the chair had grown so high that some of the clothes slid off onto the wide-board wood floor. Finally Whitney closed the closet, reached down, picked up the pile, and deposited it on the double bed where Susan was sitting.

"These will all look better on you than they do on me." Whitney said. "We're the same size. Try a couple on."

Susan stared at her and shook her head. She touched the silky fabric of a bright, patterned shirt. "But these look brand new!"

"They are."

"And this shirt would look good on you."

"It's not loud enough."

"Not loud enough?" Susan exclaimed.

Whitney laughed. "It's the wrong colors. I like reds and oranges. That's mostly blues. It'll match your eyes. And here, look at these pants, and what about this jacket? A perfect outfit. Go on." Whitney motioned toward the bathroom with her thumb. "Try them on."

Susan took the clothes and looked down at them draped in her arms. They certainly weren't like anything in *her* closet. Then she shrugged and walked to the bathroom. There was no arguing with Whitney.

When Susan came out, feeling self-conscious in clothes that were far more expensive and stylish than anything she'd ever worn, Whitney motioned her to the full-length mirror at the side of the room. Susan walked over, unsure of whether she wanted to see herself. Hesitantly she stood in front of the mirror and looked up. She almost didn't recognize the person looking back at her!

Suddenly she didn't see a collection of sharp angles and jutting bones. The image in front of her wasn't gawky. She didn't even seem so outrageously tall. "Oh . . ." was all Susan managed to get past her lips.

"Looks good, huh?" Whitney said. "See what the right clothes can do?"

"I – I guess." Susan turned slightly from one side to the other. "You really think this looks good?"

"Are you kidding? It's fantastic. But we've gotta do something with that hair. It looks like you grabbed it with one hand and cut off the ends. Come here. Sit down." Whitney was excited. She pulled out her dressing-table chair and motioned Susan into it.

"What are you going to do?" Susan said warily. "I like my hair. It's easy to take care of."

"Don't get nervous. I just want to experiment a little. There are lots of neat and flattering styles that are easy to take care of." Whitney put her hands on Susan's shoulders and turned her so she was facing the triple-faceted dressing-table mirror. Then she lifted her hands and started fluffing Susan's hair. In a flash she'd reached inside a dressing-table drawer and pulled out scissors and a comb.

"Wait a minute!" Susan said frantically. "Do you know how to cut hair?"

"Yup. If you model, you've got to learn something about it. Besides, I'm not going to do much."

"Whitney, I don't know about this."

"Wait, you'll like it." Whitney's hands were already moving rapidly, combing up pieces of hair and clipping. Susan had to admit, Whitney did *look* like she knew what she was doing. Susan hoped she really did!

"There!" Whitney said a few minutes later as she combed and fluffed out the results.

Susan brushed some itching hairs from her neck.

"Sorry, I should have put a towel around you first," Whitney said. "What do you think?"

Susan stared at her reflection and the shining brown hair that now lay in sculpted waves around her face. She liked it. It looked great! "What did you do?" she asked in wonderment.

93

"Just layered it a little, so it has more bounce."

"Wow. What a difference."

Whitney grinned. "Wait till they see you in school, in a new outfit and a new hairdo."

"I can't wear the clothes you gave me to school. They're too fancy."

"No they're not. What do you think I wear all the time? You must be a little sick of baggy jeans by now."

"I guess."

Susan changed into her regular clothes before going home. She and Whitney packed her new wardrobe in a big plastic bag, and Mrs. Duncan offered her a ride home. "I'm going into town anyway, so it won't be out of my way," she said when Susan protested. Then she cocked her hand. "What have you done with your hair? I like it."

"Whitney did it."

"Did she?" Mrs. Duncan smiled.

"See you tomorrow," Whitney called. "And make sure you wear that outfit!"

Susan's parents, of course, noticed her hair at dinner. "Whitney cut it?" Mrs. Holmes exclaimed after Susan had explained. "She's a girl of many talents. That's as good a job as you'd get in town. Very flattering."

Susan was glad when they changed the subject and started talking horses. She was getting embarrassed by all the attention. She wondered what it would be like in school tomorrow, but then Tara and her crowd probably wouldn't even notice. They usually looked right through her.

Since her bulky ski jacket covered most of her new outfit the next morning, she didn't feel too awkward when she and Whitney got off the bus. Whitney, of course, had immediately checked to make sure she was wearing it. Nobody said anything at all to her until lunchtime, when she and Whitney walked into the cafeteria together. Several of the boys, who usually ignored her totally, looked at her with puzzled frowns. When she and Whitney joined a nearly full table, Barbara White, a girl from Susan's afternoon history class, turned and smiled. "I like your outfit."

It was the first time Barbara had actually spoken to Susan except to ask about an assignment. Susan managed to stumble out a thanks. Then everyone started talking about what they were going to wear to the Christmas dance the following weekend. Susan hadn't even thought about going. She never went to dances at school – why bother, when she felt like a geek and no one would dance with her anyway? Then Whitney gave her a bright-eyed look from across the table, and Susan got a feeling that Whitney was going to try to talk her into going.

She was right. Whitney didn't say anything for the next few days, but early the following week she brought Bravo over to the farm so Susan could watch and coach her on her seat.

"Straighten your shoulders," Susan called to her. "You're slouching. That's it. Take him through the figure eight again – sitting trot."

Whitney moaned. "I hate a sitting trot. I feel like my backbone's going to break."

"You'll need to do it in any dressage test. Sit deep in the saddle – not so stiff!"

As usual Susan forgot her shyness when she was in the ring with horses. This was her element, and she knew what she was doing, although she wasn't sure she was ready to start teaching classes again. "Once more!" she called to Whitney.

Whitney made a face.

Susan laughed. "I let you cut my hair, didn't I? And I'm wearing all those clothes you gave me."

"Oh, all right." Whitney finished up, and Susan told her to give Bravo a break. Whitney dismounted and led Bravo over to where Susan was standing with Star.

"Talking about those clothes I gave you," Whitney said with a mysterious smile, "I think you should wear that dark green dress to the dance this weekend."

"I'm not going," Susan said instantly, although she knew what was coming.

"Oh yes you are. I don't want to go by myself."

"Ha! Since when are you afraid to go anywhere by yourself? I hate dances."

"Have you ever been to one?"

Susan flushed. "No," she admitted. "But I'm at least six inches taller than all the boys."

"So am I. Doesn't bother me."

"You're different," Susan said stubbornly. "I'd end up standing in a corner with no one to talk to, feeling like an absolute dork."

"You'll have me to talk to. And I don't think everyone's going to ignore you, anyway."

"What makes you say that?" Susan asked.

Whitney just smiled.

Susan frowned. Maybe with Whitney there, it wouldn't be too awful. "I'll think about it," she said.

"What did I tell you?" Whitney said gleefully as they met on the side of the dance floor in the school gym that Saturday night.

Susan was still stunned. She'd been asked for three dances in a row! They were all fast ones, but still. She couldn't believe it. And the boys who'd asked her had actually been *nice* to her. She'd even managed to dance halfway decently after Whitney's coaching for the past few afternoons. She must be dreaming!

The two girls walked to the refreshment table for a much needed drink. "Look at Tara," Whitney tee-heed. "She looks like she swallowed a frog."

Tara did look like she had an upset stomach, but Susan shrugged. "She's danced every dance."

"That's not what's bothering her. Have you looked in a mirror lately?"

"Well, yeah," Susan frowned. "I know I look different, but . . ."

"Remember the story about the ugly duckling?"

"What's that got to do with anything?"

Whitney shook her head. "Oh, never mind. The deejay's started again. And here come two more guys . . ."

Susan's feet hurt when Mrs. Duncan picked them up two hours later. As soon as she and Whitney slid into the back seat of the Jeep Cherokee, Susan took off her shoes and rubbed her sore toes. "That feels better," she said with a relieved sigh.

"So, did you girls have a good time?" Mrs. Duncan asked. "You look like it."

"Great," Whitney answered.

"Yes," Susan agreed, surprising herself with her answer, but she'd had an amazingly good time. She couldn't believe how many times she'd been asked to dance – though she couldn't imagine actually dating any of the guys she'd danced with.

"I'm glad," Mrs. Duncan said, then added. "I was wondering if you and your parents would like to join us for a Christmas Eve dinner – if you don't have plans."

"Sure," Susan said. "I mean, we usually just hand out presents to all the horses. Other than that, though, I think we're free. But my brother, Lyle, will be home too."

"Bring him along. The more the merrier. I'll give your mother a call."

"It'll be a feast." Whitney smacked her lips. "Both my parents are cooking."

Susan's parents were up when she got home, and they wanted to hear all about the dance. After she'd told them the details, feeling a little self-conscious, she mentioned Mrs. Duncan's invitation.

"Isn't that thoughtful of them," Mrs. Holmes said. "They

seem like awfully nice people. Sounds like fun. What do you think, Mitch?" she asked her husband.

"Sounds good to me. I had a talk with Morris Duncan the other day when he came to pick up Whitney. He's definitely interested in getting more horses – maybe doing some breeding."

"Whitney would like that," Susan said.

It snowed all day Christmas Eve – beautiful, powdery, fluffy snow. There was a foot on the ground by late afternoon.

"What do you say, Lyle?" Mr. Holmes said as he looked out of the kitchen window at the white landscape. The snow had stopped, and the sky was clearing. "Do you think we should get out the sleigh for our trip over to the Duncans' tonight?"

"Yes!" Susan said before her brother could answer.

Lyle grinned. "Perfect night for it."

Mr. Holmes reached for his jacket. "Okay, let's go get it ready. The Duncans might enjoy a ride after dinner."

An hour later the Holmeses, warmly bundled with blankets over their legs, set out in the four-seater sleigh. Their breath misted in the crisp, cold air. Domino, shaggy in his winter coat, was suited out in his bell-decked harness. He trotted down the drive with the eagerness of a much younger horse. The bells tinkled merrily in the white silence. The sky overhead was spattered with stars, and the glow of a three-quarter moon reflected off the snow.

"He really loves this," Susan said as Domino pulled them out of the drive and set off up the snow-covered road.

"I barely have to touch the reins." Mr. Holmes laughed from the front seat.

The moonlight was strong enough that the snow-draped pines and bare-branched hardwoods left pale shadows across the snow. In the distance Susan saw the lighted windows of the few houses on the country road. Everything was so peaceful. As they jingled up the Duncans' long, curving drive a few minutes later, Mr. Holmes circled Domino into the sweep of drive near the front door. Candles lit every window of the house, and the front light was on, displaying a bushy wreath. Before Domino had even stopped, the front door swung open and Whitney rushed out.

"Oh, wow!" she cried. "You came in a sleigh! I thought I was hearing things. I love it!"

Her parents stepped out onto the brick porch behind her. They were both smiling. "Merry Christmas! What a great surprise!" Mrs. Duncan called. "Now I really feel like I've moved to the country. Come on in."

Susan, her mother, and Lyle climbed from the sleigh. "I'll bring the horse and sleigh around back," Mr. Holmes said.

"Sure. We can find a spot for him in the barn. I'll give you a hand." Mr. Duncan eagerly hopped into the front seat beside Susan's father. Mr. Holmes slapped the reins, and Domino trotted off again.

"We can all go for sleigh rides later," Susan told Whitney as they stepped into the pine-scented warmth of the house.

"I can't wait! That's so cool!"

"If you hadn't offered, I wasn't going to give you any dinner." Mrs. Duncan laughed. "Come on into the living room. We've got the fire going, and you can meet some of our other friends."

100

She took their coats and made introductions. Soon Mr. Holmes and Mr. Duncan joined them.

The buffet dinner laid out on the big dining-room table was fabulous. Susan understood what Whitney had meant when she said they'd have a feast. Afterward they all took turns bundling up and going for sleigh rides. When everyone had had their fill and Domino was installed in the barn with a bucket of feed, they returned to the living room where the tree was sparkling and the fire blazing. Mrs. Duncan sat down at the grand piano and started to play carols, and soon everyone was singing. Susan and Whitney had already exchanged their small presents to each other. Whitney had given Susan a small silver pin of a horse and rider jumping, and Susan had found a wonderful book on eventing for Whitney.

It was nearly midnight when the Holmeses left. "Thank you!" they all said enthusiastically as they got into their coats. "It's been a wonderful night."

"For us, too. Merry Christmas!"

When Susan's family arrived home, they all went out to the barn. This visit was a Christmas Eve tradition. They gathered up bags of apples and carrots from the stable office and went from stall to stall, giving each of the horses their Christmas treat. There was a new catnip mouse each for Furball, Ralph, and Puss, and soon the air was filled with tinkling bells as the cats ecstatically rolled around with their toys.

Susan spent extra time at Star's stall, rubbing his ears and talking to him as he munched his treats. "It's going to be a good Christmas this year," she told the horse, "and next year's going to be even better. I'll be down to see you in the morning."

Susan was thrilled with the presents she received the next morning. She yelped with pleasure as she pulled out an entire new dress-riding outfit, boots to jacket.

"Thanks," she said, beaming at her parents. "I wasn't sure if you'd get me any riding stuff."

"Why?" her mother asked. "Because you didn't ride for so long this fall? We knew you'd go back when you were ready. And you'll really have something to look forward to next year with Evening Star."

"Yes. I will."

Lyle winked at her from across the room.

Right after Christmas Susan started teaching one of the beginner classes again. She'd done so much work with Star, Whitney, and Bravo that she felt confident enough now, and as long as she stayed with the beginners, she wouldn't have to rub shoulders with Tara. Tara was doing a lot of training on her own, now that she had her own horse, Dickens. Apparently she was getting so cocky that half the time she didn't want to listen to Joany or Kirin.

"I think she's making a mistake," Kirin said. "She's pushing him too fast. He may have good bloodlines and talent, but every horse needs the preliminary work."

"I know," Susan said, thinking of Star and Maxine.

Whitney was working Bravo over jumps and was eager to have Susan's advice. It was easy to advise someone about jumps when she wasn't in the saddle herself, but Susan knew it would be a different matter when she jumped Star for the first time.

"Okay, try this," Susan called. The two girls had squeezed in an hour's work in the indoor ring between two classes, but it was a bitterly cold afternoon, and their horses' breaths misted in the air. They'd both warmed up with some schooling figures, and Whitney had done a few simple jumps, but she wasn't having the best of days.

Susan had set up a crossbar, then several strides later a low parallel, then a two-fence combination, or an in-and-out, then finally, a dozen strides away, a gate. All the fences were low – not more than two feet.

"Okay, here goes," Whitney said as she trotted Bravo forward. She did fine over the early fences, but she came up too close to the second-to-last fence and popped Bravo over. That threw them out for the last fence, which he flatly refused.

"No, Whitney," Susan called. "He wasn't collected. Watch your approach. You were practically on top of the parallel before you jumped. Try it again. Look ahead to the fence and concentrate. He can't do it alone."

Whitney nodded and repeated the course. She and Bravo did a little better, but he was still in too close to the parallel, and that threw him off for the next jump. He went over this time but with absolutely no finesse.

"You're coming up to the parallel a half stride off!" Susan called.

"But I'm keeping leg on him," Whitney cried.

"Too much leg. He's a long-striding horse. You have to collect his canter and shorten up his stride so he meets the fence evenly."

Whitney looked frustrated with herself and puzzled. "I don't understand what I'm doing wrong. I was counting strides."

"He needs to shorten his stride. You have to gather him

so that he meets the fence right. He has to be a half stride farther away when he takes off. Oh, here, watch me," Susan exclaimed. "It's easier to show you than explain, and Star's a long-striding horse too." Without thinking, she trotted Star up along the outside of the first jumps. Star's ears pricked and he huffed in excitement. Susan stopped him after the combination. "This is where you land after the combination. Watch how I keep him collected." She heeled Star into a canter. "You see how he's trying to lengthen his stride? Gather the reins. You don't want to break stride – just shorten it, tighten it up." As she spoke, she held firm on Star's reins, keeping him to a shorter-strided canter. "Stride, stride, stride!" At the perfect spot, Susan squeezed her legs. Star gathered his muscles and lifted cleanly over the fence. He cantered on. Susan collected him again and sailed over the last fence, too. Then she turned him and trotted back to Whitney.

"See what I mean?" she called intently.

But Whitney was laughing.

"What's so funny? Those were perfect jumps." Susan suddenly sat straighter in the saddle and pulled Star to a sudden halt. "Oh my gosh," she gasped. "I did it! I took Star over a jump!"

"You sure did." Whitney chuckled. "And did a pretty mean-looking job of it too."

"I don't believe it . . . I did it," Susan stuttered. "And I was so afraid I'd never get up the nerve to jump again!" She leaned forward and wrapped her arms around Star's neck. He nickered in surprise. "We did it, Star. We did it!" Then she jumped from the saddle and rushed over to Whitney. The two girls hugged each other excitedly.

"Watch out, Tara. Here we come!" Whitney laughed. "Go out there and do the whole course while you're feeling so good. Star's sure ready!"

He was prancing with his head up. Susan got back in the saddle and started off. Now that she was thinking about what she was doing, she felt a little tremor of fear, but she pushed it away, concentrated on the course ahead, and came through with flying colors.

"Way to go!" Whitney cheered. "You two make us look like beginners."

"You're not, and you know it," Susan told her. "Your turn to try again."

Whitney did, and this time did everything just right. She was smiling with relief when she rode back to Susan. "I understand now. I could feel the difference."

"Good."

"Hey," Whitney added, "I almost forgot to tell you. Some people my parents do business with own some show jumpers and have a son who rides. They've invited us to a big show at Madison Square Garden this weekend. Want to come with me?"

"Madison Square Garden? That's got to be a top show."

"It is. Strictly show jumping, but it ought to be great, and we'll even be able to get a tour of the stabling area, meet all kinds of top riders."

"I'd love to go," Susan cried.

"Good. My parents and I will pick you up Saturday morning around nine. And we'll have dinner in the city too."

Susan was so excited Saturday morning; she could hardly wait for the Duncans to pick her up. It wasn't just the horse show that excited her – she'd been to plenty, though not at Madison Square Garden. It was going into New York. She'd been with her parents, of course, to go to the museums and to shop. New York City was only a couple of hours away, but her parents weren't city people and couldn't wait to get back home, away from the traffic and noise. Going with Whitney would be entirely different.

The Duncans picked her up in the BMW, and they were soon speeding their way toward Manhattan. When they reached the city proper, Mr. Duncan steered them confidently downtown through the traffic and into a parking garage by the Garden. Susan was craning her head everywhere as they walked to the entrance.

"You look like a tourist," Whitney teased.

"I am."

The Duncans' business friends, the Jordans, met them at the entrance and led them to incredible seats with a clear view of the arena below.

Whitney nudged Susan. "Will you look at those jumps!"

Susan nodded. She had been looking at the huge, tall, difficult obstacles. The course was far more difficult than anything that would be encountered in the show-jumping portion of a horse-trials competition. "Can you picture you and Bravo jumping that course?" Susan asked.

"Are you kidding?" Whitney laughed. "Well, maybe someday."

The two girls watched entranced as one spectacular horse after another entered the ring and jumped the course with a perfectly turned out rider in the saddle. Some made it look remarkably easy – effortlessly sailing over six-foot fences, smoothly maneuvering around the tight turns, horses and riders never missing a beat. It amazed Susan. Others had trouble with knocked-down poles and refusals, which cost them valuable points. The horses and riders were also working against the clock. Those with clear rounds – and there were several – would win on the basis of the best time.

"I can't believe there were five clear rounds!" Susan exclaimed to Whitney.

"Yeah, but these guys are the tops in the country, remember – horses and riders."

Susan shook her head as she watched the last competitors finish the course. Could she and Star ever jump a course this difficult? Yes, she decided after a moment, they could. With practice, of course. Star was definitely in the same league as many of the horses she'd seen jumping, although all of them had been in training much longer than Star, who was a youngster at four. Of the horses that had gone clean, none was younger than eight.

Moments later, when the winner was announced, Susan and Whitney turned to each other and smiled. Lisa Colwin, on a beautiful big dapple gray nine-year old, Whiteberg, had been far and away the best.

"He looks like Star." Whitney grinned.

Susan laughed. "No wonder I wanted them to win!"

Then the Jordans took them all behind the scenes. Susan felt shivers of excitement just being near some of the riders and horses. The Jordans introduced them to their son, Andrew, who'd been competing for only a few years and was pretty happy with an eighth-place finish.

"Eighth out of thirty competitors isn't bad," he said, smiling. As they talked, a couple of other young riders came over. Whitney, of course, was gabbing away a mile a minute. Susan was content just to listen and take it all in, but one really cute blond-haired boy in his mid-teens came over and introduced himself as Ronny Anderson. She told him her name, then immediately flushed shyly.

He misunderstood her blush. "You must be remembering my ride," he said. "Pretty awful, but I don't usually compete in show jumping. Andrew talked me into trying, but my love is eventing."

"No . . . I mean I don't remember your ride . . . I mean . . ." Susan stopped. She was going from bad to worse. "I like eventing too," she said in a rush.

"You ride?" he asked.

She nodded. "I'm training a horse now. I hope we'll be ready for some of the spring trials."

"Where do you ride?"

"New England, mostly. My family has a stable in Connecticut."

"Oh, yeah? I'll be competing in New England this spring too."

Their conversation jumped ahead from there. Ronny wanted to know about her horse, then described his own. They talked about the ups and downs of training and conditioning and the upcoming horse trials. Susan had no idea how much time had passed until Whitney walked over.

"Hate to break this up," she said with a smile, "but if we're going to eat, we've got to go."

"Oh, right," Susan said. She blushed again. She hated those embarrassing flushes, but no one seemed to notice.

"Great talking to you," Ronny said. "Maybe I'll see you at some of the spring meets. Good luck with your training."

"Same to you," Susan said, uncertainly smiling a good-bye and following Whitney.

"What's this?" Whitney teased as soon as they were out of earshot. "Who is he?"

Susan blushed all over again. "Ronny Anderson. He rode today. We were just talking about horses and eventing."

"Uh-huh," Whitney said with twinkling eyes.

Susan came back from the horse show fired with enthusiasm. Watching the top riders had inspired her, and Star was willing and eager. He was ready for anything, always trying his best. Susan was thrilled, but she'd always believed in his talent.

Whitney and Susan worked as hard as they could. Since the weather was now so unpredictable, Whitney left Bravo at Shadowbrook Farm several days a week so she and Susan could train together. She paid a boarding fee, too. "My parents don't mind," she said. "They're glad I'm doing this, and there's nowhere to train at our place with all the ice and snow. Besides, I've got a couple of modeling assignments coming up on the weekends. You want any more clothes?"

"I haven't worn all the ones you gave me yet," Susan answered.

"I'll check out what's around in your colors."

Susan and Star progressed rapidly, from hopping over raised cavalletti, to a few simple fences, to a whole course of varied jumps. It was a retraining program for both of them, building confidence in each. Susan didn't need to hear Whitney's words of praise to know she and Star were doing well.

They had other curious visitors too. Kirin and Joany seemed to slip into the indoor ring more often than usual, going home late just to watch. Susan's parents were in and out.

Susan was a wreck at first when others were watching. She hadn't lost her fear of making a stupid mistake. But Star seemed to know when her concentration wasn't at its best, and did the right thing on his own. Eventually, though, she got used to the watchers and managed to forget them.

"I can't believe this is the same horse I rode this fall!" Lyle told her when he watched them practice one weekend in February. "His mind's completely on business. He's putting his heart into it. I'd never have guessed he had this much talent. What the heck did you do?"

"I don't know exactly," Susan answered, which was the truth. "I haven't done anything different than you or Mom or Kirin did. You're all super riders."

"He trusts her," Whitney said.

Lyle studied the horse, then nodded. "You hear about these cases where an animal forms a special bond – a one-on-one sort of thing. Whatever it is, I'm glad it happened. You and this horse are going to go places, Brat."

"We haven't gone much beyond beginner stuff yet," Susan protested.

"This horse has class – now that he's decided to show it. I can't wait to see him on the cross-country course. Keep up the good work," he said as he left the ring.

⭐ 9

On a chilly February afternoon, Susan and Whitney led the
horses into the ring after one of Kirin's classes to find a set
of gymnastic fences set up.

"Hey, great," Whitney said. "Something new! Why
haven't we tried this before?"

Because just the sight of the series of fences had Susan's
head reeling. She couldn't believe her reaction. In her
mind she was back in Jocko's saddle, roaring through
the gymnastics, losing control before the last two jumps,
botching those, losing her stirrup and crashing over the
schooling-ring fence. They were in the indoor ring – but the
course was set up almost exactly the same, including the
two jumps after the gymnastic.

Suddenly she couldn't breathe. An icy finger licked down
her spine. She'd known for weeks that Star and Bravo would
benefit from some gymnastic work, but she'd deliberately
put it off, afraid that she might react exactly as she was now.

"What's wrong?" Whitney was staring at her with a
worried scowl. "You all right?"

Susan briskly shook her head, trying to clear it. "Yes . . . yes. Nothing's wrong." But her words came out with a tremble.

"You going to try the gymnastics?" Kirin's voice called from behind them.

Susan jumped, but Whitney answered brightly. "It looks like fun. We haven't done this before."

"You haven't?" Kirin said in surprise. "Susan, you must be slipping," she joked.

Susan just stared at the series of jumps. She'd have to try them – she had no excuse not to. *I'll be all right*, she told herself. She wouldn't be riding a green horse this time; Star would get her through. Still, her jaw muscle quivered as she explained the gymnastic to Whitney. "It'll be a lot like jumping a two-fence combination. The fences are close. You'll land, and you'll immediately jump again. Keep thinking of the rhythm," she told her friend. "Jump, land, squeeze, jump."

"Gotcha," Whitney said as she gathered her reins, turned Bravo, and trotted him toward the low first crossbar.

Susan went to the side of the series. She refused to think about Star and herself jumping the same obstacles. "Squeeze!" Susan coached encouragingly as Whitney landed between each progressively higher fence. "Squeeze!"

Whitney was listening, and Bravo did his best, carrying them through, just ticking the last fence rail with his hind feet.

"I didn't squeeze hard enough at the last fence," Whitney said breathlessly as she rode over. "I kept thinking how big it was."

112

"You'll know next time," Susan said.

"Your turn," Whitney said, grinning. "I can't wait to see you and Star do this!"

Susan hoped she could live up to Whitney's expectations. She couldn't let herself think about what had happened the last time she'd jumped a gymnastic. She and Star just had to go out and do it. "Help me with this, boy," she whispered to the horse, then took a deep breath and trotted him around the top of the ring toward the crossbar. Her head was up, her eyes focused forward between Star's ears. Then she heard the indoor ring door slam. She glanced toward it.

Tara was entering the ring. For an instant Susan froze, but it was too late to stop their approach to the jump. Star was ready to go, and she'd look like an idiot if she pulled him up.

Just think of the course, she told herself. *Forget Tara*! But her concentration had snapped. Panic gripped her. Her legs suddenly seemed weak as she and Star trotted toward the first crossbar, then started surging through the gymnastic. It was Star who carried them through, not his rider. She tried to keep the rhythm of the gymnastic . . . squeeze, jump . . . land . . . but her brain was like cotton, her muscles like putty. Star valiantly lifted them both over the first three fences, but Susan didn't give him enough leg over the fourth. He rapped the fence and landed awkwardly. Susan automatically steadied him, but she knew it would take a miracle to get them over the last fence. Star knew it too and skidded to a sudden stop. Susan gasped as she went flying sideways out of the saddle to land at the foot of the jump. The soft dirt cushioned her fall, but her heart was pounding. She wasn't hurt, but she saw how close she'd come to landing on the jump itself.

Shaking slightly, she slowly gathered her legs under her and stood. One hand still gripped Star's rein. He was looking down at her with apology in his soft brown eyes.

"It wasn't your fault," she managed to whisper, but beyond that she couldn't move. She was terrified. And Tara had seen it all – just like before.

"Get back up on him! Now!" Kirin shouted loudly from the side of the ring. "Take him around and do those jumps again! Now, Susan!"

Kirin was using her instructor's voice. At the commanding tone, Susan didn't think, just automatically reacted. She led Star a few feet from the jump, threw the reins back over his head, and mounted. In a daze she saw Whitney's worried expression. Kirin was standing with her hands on her hips like a general. Susan refused to look at Tara. How was she going to do it? She was trembling so badly, she could barely hold the reins. She'd never get through the gymnastics again.

Then Star craned his head around and whickered softly. She swallowed. "You think we can do it, boy? You still believe in me after that mess?" Again Star whickered.

Susan closed her eyes, took a deep breath, and straightened her shoulders. "All right. Let's go." As they trotted to the end of the ring, Susan's head suddenly started to clear. She felt a surge of determination. She was still shaken, and Tara was still watching. But she knew she had an incredible horse beneath her, and she wasn't going to fail this time.

She was nearly herself again as she put Star into a trot

114

and circled the end of the ring. She was tuned to the horse; she could feel his willingness through the reins. Her head was up, looking ahead to the first low X. They flitted over, Susan immediately gave Star leg and they soared over the next and the next of the increasingly higher jumps – landing, soaring, landing, soaring. To Susan, Star felt like he had wings on his heels. She knew they must have cleared the last jumps with a foot to spare even before she heard Kirin and Whitney cheering.

Star tossed his head as Susan circled him and brought him back down to a trot. She looked over in time to see Tara stomping from the ring, then leaned down and hugged Star's neck. "Thanks, Star . . . thanks so much."

In a moment she rode over to where Kirin and Whitney were standing, smiling at the side of the ring. "I'm glad you yelled at me," she told Kirin.

"You *had* to get right back up." Kirin said. "If you hadn't, you would have lost your nerve again."

"You knew . . . about my losing my nerve?"

"I guessed. It happens to all of us at some time or other."

"Thanks," Susan said.

Susan and Whitney knew that time was running short. Spring was around the corner, and they still couldn't try the cross-country course. They practiced dressage in the middle of the ring – walking, trotting, and cantering the horses as fluidly as possible through the required figures. When horse and rider were working well together at dressage, the rider's aides should be all but invisible to observers. The horse should respond instantly, with the rider quiet in the saddle.

Afterward they practiced the jumps set up around the perimeter of the ring.

Then in mid-March the weather suddenly changed. The temperatures warmed – and stayed warm. Susan and Whitney could start practicing on the cross-country course. Susan had ridden all of the beginner fences before on her Morgan, but this was a completely different situation. Star hadn't been ridden over a cross-country course since Maxine had had him. Susan was uncertain how he would react, but after some initial fidgeting, he settled down, and they started simply. She and Whitney jumped the low side of the fences, choosing obstacles that were similar to the fences they'd jumped in the ring – single logs, split-rail fences, a hedge. Then they tried a narrow ditch, a jump up to the top of a bank, a stride, and a jump down. And Susan, remembering Star's experience with Maxine, started getting him used to water.

A narrow brook threaded its way through the property. A jump had been constructed incorporating the brook, and in another section of the course, the brook had been dammed and a railroad tie set into each bank so a horse had to jump down into the water and out again. But Susan wasn't about to attempt those yet. She wanted Star to get used to the sight of the water and to jumping over a narrow stretch of it.

"Here," she told Whitney. "Try this with Bravo, too. There's a nice grassy approach on both sides, and the brook's really narrow." She walked Star up to the water and let him have a good look. "See, just some wet stuff. Nothing to be frightened of." When she thought he'd had a good enough look, she turned him, walked him several yards away, then turned again and trotted him toward the brook. As they neared its edge, she squeezed with her legs. "Over!" she called.

Star jumped, a little hesitantly, but he was over and cantering on the grass of the opposite side. "Good boy!" she praised. "See, it's not so bad once you know what you're doing. Let's try it from the other side."

Susan repeated the exercise, and this time Star went over much less hesitantly. She took him over several more times until he was completely comfortable; then she told Whitney to try it.

Bravo had no problems with water, and hopped over without a quiver.

"This isn't as hard as I thought," Whitney said as they finished up a few minutes later.

"Well, it'll get harder," Susan said, but her cheeks were glowing. It had gone much better than she'd expected. The bigger obstacles that they'd eventually have to jump didn't seem so daunting anymore. She vigorously rubbed Star's neck. "You're doing great, sweetie! So are you, Bravo."

"I hope this nice weather stays around for a while," Whitney added as they left the wooded trails for the meadow. "I want to get in all the practice I can."

When they arrived back at the stable, Tara and Kirin were arguing outside the barn. Tara was holding the reins of her horse, and he was tacked up and ready to go. She was itching to go out on the course.

"You've never ridden the course before, Tara," Kirin said firmly.

"I've walked it."

"I can't let you go out there alone."

117

Tara shot an angry look at Susan and Whitney. "You let them ride the course."

"Susan's had experience. She knows what she's doing." To say nothing of the fact her parents owned the farm. She could do what she wanted, Susan thought dryly.

"Oh, sure," Tara sneered.

"Look, the jumps are entirely different, and there'll be more to distract your horse. It's new territory for him."

"I'm not worried," Tara said arrogantly. She turned and brushed past Susan and Whitney, then mounted and rode toward the meadow.

"I'd better tell your father," Kirin said to Susan. "He's not going to like it. Then again, it might serve her right if she has a spill. She needs a little wind taken out of her sails."

"She could get hurt." Susan thought it would serve Tara right too, but the farm couldn't take the risk.

Kirin made a face. "All right, I'll saddle one of the school horses and go after her. She's just lucky I haven't got a class."

As Kirin strode off angrily, Whitney gave Susan a look. Then they both started to giggle. "We're awful," Susan said, laughing.

"No, we're not. How can you say that after the things Tara's said and done to you?"

"All the same, I don't want her to get hurt," Susan said.

"Well, she *is* a good rider," Whitney admitted reluctantly. "And Kirin will bring her back."

Susan nodded.

Of course, nothing happened to Tara that day.

The warm weather continued to hold out, though there were a few spring showers. Susan and Whitney went out on the cross-country course every chance they got. They were improving, trying more and more difficult jumps, often returning mud spattered but cheerful.

Everyone at the stable was feeling a lift in their spirits. There were entry forms for the spring shows spread all over the battered office desk. Kirin, Joany, and Susan's parents were busily talking about who should enter which show and when.

"Yes, I know Señor's coming along," Joany said to Kirin, "but I think I'll enter him at the training level for now. It'll give his confidence a boost to be able to handle the course so easily. That means you and I won't be competing against each other."

"No," Kirin said, laughing. "I'll be competing against the Wertheimer snob next door. Is that why you're staying at training level?"

"Be serious," Joany shot back. "Hey, Susan, what shows are you entering this year?"

"I'm not sure. I don't think we're ready yet."

"Who says?" Kirin questioned. "You two are doing great. You won't have any trouble with dressage, and he's eating up the jumps."

"I haven't spent enough time on cross-country."

"A few more weeks' practice will fix that. The Hunt Club has something scheduled in early April – only show jumping. I guess they were afraid their cross-country course wouldn't be ready. Perfect for you. You've got to enter."

Susan hesitated. The small show *would* be a perfect prep

for her and Star. Star was ready. She wasn't so sure about herself.

Whitney walked up behind her. "Well, *I'll* enter." She gave Susan a challenging look.

"Tara's going to be competing," Joany said.

"Oh?"

"It's time you and Star showed her up," Whitney told her. Both Kirin and Joany were grinning at her.

Susan made up her mind. She had to start showing again sometime, and if she didn't enter, Tara would only have more to talk about. "Okay, but I'm only entering in intermediate."

"Sounds reasonable." Kirin nodded. "You and Star haven't competed together before. It'll be good practice. Tara's riding in intermediate too."

"Go get her!" Whitney laughed.

Susan and Whitney had practiced like crazy preparing for the show, but Susan was a bundle of nerves as they left on Saturday morning for the Hunt Club in the Holmeses' family car. Mr. Holmes, Lyle, and Joany had already gone ahead with the van of horses that would be competing. Whitney's parents would meet them there. Susan and Whitney slid into the backseat. Kirin and Mrs. Holmes were in front. Their dress outfits and hard hats were wrapped in plastic and carefully placed in the trunk of the car.

"I don't know if I should have entered," Susan said quietly to Whitney.

"I noticed Tara was looking good yesterday," Whitney said.

"Hmm. I hope we do all right, Whit."

"What are you two worrying about?" Mrs. Holmes called from behind the wheel. "You've both been riding beautifully. Your horses are in top shape, and Susan, you should be entered in advanced, not intermediate."

"Your mother's right," Kirin agreed. "Tara's good, but so are you. Just give it your best shot, and you'll both do fine."

Susan gazed out the window at the rolling countryside and wished she could feel so confident. Daffodils were blooming, and the leaves were starting to come out on the trees in a misty green. The weather couldn't have been better for the show – a warm day for early April, without a cloud in the sky. Star had been raring to go that morning, and it wasn't as if Susan hadn't ridden in shows before – and done well. There was a wall of blue ribbons in her bedroom. But this was her first time in the show ring after her accident. She felt like she had a lot to live up to.

Whitney looked over and gave her a reassuring smile.

"Aren't you nervous at all?" Susan asked.

"Oh, a little, but I'm not expecting to get a first."

A few minutes later Mrs. Holmes pulled into the tree-bordered Hunt Club drive. As they neared the clubhouse and stables at the top of the hill, they saw that one whole pasture was filled with vans. People and horses were everywhere.

Mrs. Holmes pulled into a spot at the end of a long line of cars. "We should have gotten here sooner. I didn't think it would be this crowded, but I guess we're not the only ones ready to start competing again after the winter."

As they climbed out, Lyle came jogging across the grass. "I saw you coming. We're over there under the trees. Here, let me help," he added as Mrs. Holmes opened the trunk and reached for a cooler and picnic hamper. "We might as well leave the clothes here until it's time to change."

"I wonder where my parents are," Whitney said. "I'll be lucky to find them."

"We'll have time to walk around," Susan told her. "There's still an hour before the beginner and pony classes begin."

They set out across the grass and soon reached the big van. Susan saw Tara approaching from the opposite direction. They'd vanned her horse, Dickens, over as well.

Mr. Holmes waved when he saw them. "We should get the horses out and walk them around a little before everyone registers. Lyle, why don't you start bringing them out?" For the next few minutes they were all busy as Lyle led the seven horses from the van. Susan and Whitney took Star and Bravo and walked them under the trees. Then the horses would go back in the van again until it was time to warm them up. Star and Bravo looked around eagerly at their surroundings, snorting as other horses' calls echoed through the air.

"Easy, Star," Susan said. "Don't get too excited yet. We've got a ways to go."

"I can't keep it straight," Whitney said. "Who's riding in which classes?"

"You, me and Tara in junior intermediate. My father in the hunter division. Everyone else in advanced. And Joany's not riding because Señor bruised his foot."

"Gotcha. We'll have a lot of people to watch."

After the horses were back in the van, everyone walked up to the clubhouse to register and get their numbers. Susan saw a lot of people she knew from other shows, including Maxine Wertheimer, who was talking with some other riders. Maxine didn't see her, but she probably wouldn't have recognized Susan if she had. Susan pointed out the slender, dark-haired girl to Whitney.

"So that's Star's old owner? I wonder what horse she's riding today."

"Probably the same one she rode at Ledyard in the fall. From what Kirin and Joany said, he was well trained and experienced before Maxine got him."

"So she'll do well."

"She almost always does, but she'll be riding in junior advanced. We won't have to worry about her."

They collected their numbers and finally found Whitney's parents. "Here you are!" Mrs. Duncan called, hurrying over. "We've been looking all over."

"Some kind of crowd, isn't it?" Whitney grinned. "The van's over here. Come on. Susan and I have to get our stuff and change."

Susan's parent's, Joany and Kirin were at the van, seated in the sunshine on the deck chairs they'd brought. They were chatting with some friends who were also competing. Lyle had wandered off to check out horses and see some of his own friends.

Susan's parents welcomed the Duncans warmly. "Come and sit down," Mrs. Holmes said. "I was just going to break open the picnic basket. Let me introduce you."

Tara strolled up as Mrs. Holmes was making introductions. She was already dressed in gleaming boots, white breeches, and white shirt and stock, although she carried her jacket and hard hat in her hands. When Kirin saw her, she got up and walked over.

"I'm going to start warming Dickens up," Tara said. "Can you keep an eye on my jacket and number?"

"Put them in the cab of the van," Kirin told her, then glanced at her watch. "You really don't have to start warming up yet. The beginner classes are just starting. You have plenty of time."

"No," Tara answered stubbornly. "I want to do it now, before the warm-up jumps get too crowded."

Kirin shrugged. "Go ahead, then."

Tara left her jacket and number on the seat of the van, put her hard hat over her neatly French-braided blond hair, and went into the van to get Dickens. Susan frowned to herself. Was it possible Miss Know-it-all was feeling a little nervous?

While Tara was tacking up Dickens, Susan and Whitney went to get their clothes to change. The Hunt Club had huge changing rooms, but they were mobbed. Susan and Whitney found a corner in the crowd of chatting women and got into their habits and boots.

"Whoa," Whitney said, "this is worse than the dressing rooms at some of the modeling studios." Whitney didn't seem the least embarrassed stripping down to her underwear in front of everyone, but Susan hated it and kept her back toward the others. Whitney managed to squeeze in front of one of the mirrors to check that everything was on straight, and they headed back to the van to get Star and Bravo.

The horses definitely knew something was going on as the girls tacked them up. They pranced and whickered to each other, touching noses and whuffing excitedly. The two were old friends now, after all the hours they'd spent training together.

Susan had almost forgotten her nervousness, but now she was feeling twinges again.

"Don't you girls want to have something to eat before you warm up?" Susan's mother asked.

"Not me," Susan said. Her stomach was jumpy enough. Whitney grabbed a sandwich.

"We'll be at the ring well before your class starts," Mrs. Holmes added.

The girls led the horses off to the warm-up area behind the show ring. There was a crowd of spectators around the ring and in the bleachers that had been set up along one side. The pony classes were in progress.

"You've ridden here before," Whitney said. "What do you think the course is going to be like?"

"They change it every time. There'll be a lot of mixed jumps – parallels, gates, combinations, brush. And I know there'll be some kind of a spread, maybe more than one. They might even rig up a water jump, though it probably won't be more than a water-filled ditch. We'll get a chance to walk the course beforehand."

A lot of riders were using the warm-up fences, but fortunately the Hunt Club had set up more than just a couple. As Susan and Whitney mounted, they saw Tara coming down one line of jumps.

"I hope she hasn't been at it all this time," Susan said. "She'll burn him out before they get in the ring."

"Do you care?" Whitney asked.

Susan hesitated. "Well . . ."

"Boy, you're a softy." Whitney laughed, shaking her head.

They warmed up Star and Bravo by trotting and cantering them around the field near the jumps, then took their turns going over the fences. The warm-up fences weren't difficult. Their purpose was to get the horses and riders limbered and ready for the ring. But Susan noticed the extra spring as Star

126

leaped over the obstacles. He was enthusiastic, excited. She hoped he wasn't too excited. "Good!" Susan praised him as she rode him away from the jumps. She saw that Whitney and Bravo were doing great too.

Then she glanced to her side, behind the ropes surrounding the warm-up area, and saw Maxine Wertheimer. Maxine was in white breeches and shirt. Her short black hair and polished black boots gleamed in the sunlight. She was staring at Star, her forehead furrowed in puzzlement. Then she climbed over the ropes and walked right up to Susan.

"Is this Evening Star?" she demanded.

"Yes," Susan said.

Maxine looked up at her. Until then she'd been looking only at Star, who was starting to fidget and blow uneasily through his nose. "I used to own this horse," Maxine said. "Do I know you?"

"Susan Holmes."

"Holmes . . ." Maxine frowned. "Shadowbrook Farm, next door."

"Right."

"We sold him to you as a stable horse. He was a dud. You mean you're going to try and show him?"

"Yes, we are," Susan answered. "He isn't a dud." Susan hated the little smirk on Maxine's face and wished she had the nerve to tell Maxine that her training methods stank. But this wasn't the time or place.

"Actually, he can probably handle this dinky course all right. It won't be much of a challenge. But he'll never make an eventing horse." With that, Maxine turned on her heel and strode off.

127

That shows how much you know, you idiot! Susan silently yelled at Maxine's retreating figure. She patted Star's neck soothingly. "It's okay, boy." Star had gotten more and more jittery as Maxine had stood talking. Now he was prancing and snorting nervously. "She can't bother you anymore. You're mine now."

Whitney and Bravo trotted up. Whitney's eyes were dancing with curiosity. She motioned with a nod of her head toward Maxine. "So what did *she* have to say?"

"She recognized Star."

"And?"

"Told me he was a loser."

Whitney chuckled deep in her throat. "Won't she be surprised."

"She doesn't think much of today's show – said it wasn't really a challenge. So I doubt she'll be very impressed if we do well."

"What do you mean *if?*" Whitney said. "You're going to."

Susan sighed. "I hope."

The beginners' classes had finished. Crews were already working frantically in the jump ring, changing the course. Susan felt her heart pounding. It was almost time for their class. Whitney looked over. "Don't let her get you uptight."

That was easy to say, but it was suddenly very important to Susan that Maxine see the caliber of Star's talent. She knew the horse wouldn't have any trouble. She just prayed she wouldn't let him down herself.

The Holmeses, the Duncans, and Kirin met them outside the ring as the entrants in the junior intermediate class gathered outside.

"Joany says to wish you luck," Kirin said. "She's staying

at the van to watch the horses, but she knows you're both going to do great. Tara too," she added, although Tara was standing too far away to hear.

"Let me help tie on your number." Mrs. Holmes told Susan, taking the cardboard square and holding it in place as Susan tied the strings. Her mother gave Susan's shoulders a comforting squeeze and said softly, "I can already see the blue ribbon hanging off his bridle."

"Thanks, Mom." *She must have guessed how nervous I am*, Susan thought.

Whitney walked over. "Time to walk the course," she said. For all her denials, Whitney was looking pretty nervous herself.

Susan pushed every other thought from her mind as her competitors walked into the ring. It was a fairly difficult course for intermediate. It started with an easy railed fence, but a sharp left turn to a double gate followed; then back right again to a wishing well, forward to a long spread, off it to a combination, left again to a wall, then a brush. It ended by circling back to an oxer of poles over a double wall base, then three big jumps two strides apart to the end.

"I don't know if I can do this," Whitney said.

"You can do it. We've jumped harder stuff at the farm. The only difference is that we'll have people competing against us here. Just stay alert and keep on your toes." Susan wished she felt as sure as her words.

The entrants left the ring, and a few minutes later the announcer called the first rider. It was a big class, with nearly twenty competitors. Susan was just thankful she wasn't the first to go. That was always the hardest. Later riders could watch for where difficulties arose and be prepared before they got in the ring.

Susan, Whitney, and the other waiting riders walked their horses up and down to keep them limber. Susan couldn't help wondering what was going through everyone's mind. Some of the riders looked incredibly relaxed, but you never knew.

Tara was number five. Tara's parents must have been around somewhere, but Susan hadn't seen them. She and Whitney moved a little closer to the ring to watch. There was no arrogant smile on Tara's face today. She was intent and frowning, but she and Dickens went through cleanly until the last fence, when Dickens ticked the top rail and took it down.

"She didn't give him enough leg through that last combination," Whitney whispered to Susan.

"Those last fences are giving everyone trouble. That's a tight turn coming into them, and it's hard to build up enough momentum. But Tara and Dickens are the best so far."

Three more riders went; then it was Whitney's turn to mount. "You'll do great," Susan said, giving her a hug. "Good luck!" Whitney rode out into the ring.

Susan held her breath as Whitney went through. Whitney was timing everything perfectly, bringing Bravo in to correct takeoff points, giving him plenty of leg over the jump. They looked impressive and were clear until the oxer. Bravo didn't extend enough and knocked down one of the poles over the wall base. Susan knew Whitney must have been looking ahead to the troublesome last three fences and hadn't thought enough about the fence they were jumping. She hadn't given Bravo enough leg. Now she was tied with

Tara, who'd had only one fault. But the knocked down pole had unsettled Whitney enough that she rushed a little going into the last three fences. Bravo was extending but not lifting enough. His rear hoofs rapped the top rail on the last fence, and they got their second fault.

"Oh, darn it," Whitney said as she slid out of the saddle. She looked terribly disappointed. "I know what I did wrong. You don't have to tell me. I was thinking about those last three fences . . . and we'd been doing so well!"

"You did fine!" Susan assured her. "You looked fantastic, right on – and two faults isn't exactly bad."

Whitney sighed as she pulled up Bravo's stirrups. "Yeah, I know, but I wanted to at least tie Tara."

"This is your first show on Bravo," Susan reminded her.

"It's her first show on Dickens, too."

There wasn't anything Susan could say to that.

Susan had to wait for three more riders to jump before she went out. All the while she was taking deep breaths, mentally talking herself up to do it well. She didn't even care about beating Tara anymore. She just wanted to give Star the ride he deserved, show off his talent for everyone to see.

The rider before her was called, and Susan was told to prepare. Her hands felt like ice; her knees trembled as she pulled down Star's stirrups, checked them over, and mounted. Star was definitely ready. He was dancing beneath her with ears pricked. Friends and family were wishing her good luck, but Susan barely heard. The previous rider left the ring. Susan trotted Star in.

"Please help me, sweetie," she told Star. "You're going to have to get us through. I can't think straight."

Star's ears were back, listening. He whuffed softly as Susan stopped him long enough to nod to the judges. Then she paused, took a deep breath, and put Star into a canter. Looking ahead to the first jump, Susan headed him toward it. Star took them over, and after that Susan clicked in automatically. Now her mind was totally on the course and the horse beneath her. As they landed, she immediately looked left to the next fence. One of the difficulties of the show ring was remembering the order and sequence of the jumps; they weren't set out in a comfortable circle. Susan tightened her left rein and collected Star. He hadn't had a chance to walk the course; this was all new to him. His performance depended upon her giving him the correct aides and signals. They flew over the double gate, Susan stretching over Star's neck in perfect balance. She turned him right to the wishing well, and they surged forward to the long spread. Her legs were tight on his sides as they lifted; her arms stretched along his neck, allowing him to extend. They breezed through the combination, soared over the wall. *We're working together*, Susan thought. *We're a team.* One, two, three strides, squeeze, and they were over the brush. A tight circle left to the oxer. Star must have had half a foot to spare as he cleared it. Now the last three fences. Susan had been watching the other riders. They'd all cut the right-hand turn as tightly as they could, trying to save timing points. Susan put in an extra stride, bringing Star out a little wider so that their approach to the series of three jumps was straighter. Off the curve, one, two, squeeze, jump . . . one, two, squeeze, jump . . . one, two, squeeze *hard*, jump.

Star was over and landed, and there was no sound of a

132

fallen rail. They'd done it! They'd gone a clean round – the first clean round!

Susan was stunned. She knew they'd cleared the course, but she didn't realize how impressively until they rode out of the ring. Her family and friends and the spectators in the stands were cheering.

There were three more riders. Susan had to wait, but none of them went clean. Star stood proudly a few minutes later when the top riders were called into the ring. His head was high as one of the judges walked over to attach his first blue ribbon to his bridle, and Susan felt ready to burst with joy. They'd done it. Together she and Star had done it! But this was just the beginning.

"What a day!" Kirin cried from the front seat when they left the Hunt Club late that afternoon. "I know I got beaten, but look who I took a second to!" She laughed and looked over at Mr. Holmes.

Susan had noticed her mother was almost looking like a teenager, she was so pleased. "I admit we did well," she said, "but half the credit goes to Passion. I'm just sorry Lyle had trouble with Sir George."

"I'm not," Kirin teased. "I know they would have beaten me if Sir George hadn't been in a cranky mood."

"He sure was temperamental, wasn't he?" Whitney said. "What was wrong with him?"

"Horses get their moods just like everyone else," Mrs. Holmes answered. "Too bad that he picked today to be cantankerous."

"I guess I'm pretty happy with my tie for third after all," Whitney added.

"You should be," Kirin said. "You just got a little anxious about those last three fences. Otherwise, it was a perfect ride, and we all live and learn."

"Poor Tara looked like she was going to cry after she knocked down that pole," Mrs. Holmes said sympathetically. "She's really taking this seriously, isn't she? Maybe too seriously."

Kirin shrugged. "She's been going at it all right, but I think she started warming up Dickens too early. They were both past their peak when they finally got on the course."

Strangely enough, Susan felt a stab of sympathy for Tara too. It was weird, after all the nasty things Tara had done to Susan in the past, but getting back at Tara didn't seem important anymore. She knew Tara had been trying her hardest to win. All that mattered to Susan was making as much progress with Star over the next few weeks as possible. Their victory had cemented her confidence in both herself and the horse.

"Well, there will be plenty of other shows," Mrs. Holmes said. "Is Tara interested in competing in any horse trials, or does she want to stick with show jumping?"

"She's been out on the cross-country course," Kirin answered.

"Looks like Shadowbrook is going to have a busy spring and summer."

On Monday afternoon Susan, Whitney, Kirin, and Joany gathered in the stable office before classes began to look carefully over the spring schedule.

"I know your father is going to the Winter Farm Horse Trials in Connecticut later this month," Joany said. "He, Kirin, and I are competing."

Susan had been to the Winter Farm trials the year before and knew they would be a good starting point for her and

135

Star. The course was only moderately demanding, and the top riders wouldn't be competing.

"Then there's the University of New Hampshire Trials the first weekend in May, Three Oaks Farm in Massachusetts the weekend after, and a Vermont show the next weekend. Then there's Shepley the first weekend in June . . . and of course, Groton the end of June. That's the icing on the cake, but we'll all have to be at our peak to do well at Groton."

Susan twirled her hat in her hands, thinking. Groton was one of the biggest of the New England horse trials, second only to Ledyard, and it gained in reputation every year. She and Jasmine had competed at the novice level the year before and done well, especially considering Susan had almost outgrown the Morgan mare. But if she and Star were going to compete this year, they'd better get cracking.

"Is it too late to send in an entry for Winter Farm?" she asked. "It's only two weeks away."

"Not if we send in a late-entry fee." Kirin said. She dug through a pile of forms on the desk. "Here we go. I can fill them out for you. What about you, Whitney?"

"I don't know if I'm going to enter this one."

"Why not? You'll enter in novice, and believe me, most of the riders at Winter Farm aren't going to be any better than you. If it'll make you feel any better, I'll come out with you and Susan on the cross-country course today."

"Would you?"

"We may be sorry." Susan grinned. "Kirin's like a drill sergeant out there."

"I'm not like that at all!" Kirin protested.

"Wanna bet?" Joany laughed, shaking her blond head.

"But you get results. Your students are too afraid of you to do anything but a good job."

"Humph," Kirin grouched, then looked over at Whitney and Susan. "Go get tacked up. I'll fill out the entry forms and meet you outside the barn."

"What are you worried about?" Susan quietly asked Whitney as they entered the stable.

"Not like me, is it?" Whitney admitted with a smile. "I'm just thinking about the size of those big cross-country jumps."

"Oh, you won't have to jump anything like those, not in novice. The fences won't be any harder than the ones we've been practicing on, though we're both going to have to put in some work before the trials – not just on cross-country, but on dressage and the show fences."

And work they did, every single afternoon and on the weekends. They varied their practice sessions, some days riding cross-country, and practicing dressage and show jumping in the indoor ring when the weather was rainy. Tara was working equally hard, though she wasn't entering the Winter Farm trials. She was aiming for the next show. She avoided Susan and Whitney at the stables, but at school Tara couldn't resist putting in a little dig once in a while.

"Of course Susan's bound to improve," Susan heard her say to a friend who'd been to the Hunt Club show. "She gets all the special help she needs and can ride whenever she wants. It's the horse that carries her through, anyway."

Most of the time Susan was so preoccupied with her riding and Star's progress that she didn't even notice, but Whitney did.

"She's jealous." Whitney giggled.

"Of me?" Susan quizzed. "Be serious."

"Oh, I am. You really walk around in a daze sometimes. It still bugs Tara that you're doing so well on the horse she wanted to buy. And don't you notice the way some of the guys have been looking at you?"

"They've always given me funny looks," Susan said, although she did realize that some of the boys in class had grown during the school year. She didn't tower over all of them like she had in the fall, but she hadn't forgotten the way they'd ignored her then.

"Oh, never mind," Whitney laughed.

The Friday afternoon before the show, Susan and Whitney took the horses through everything. Kirin had come along to watch, riding beside them through cross-country, then standing by the outdoor ring as they took the horses through the required dressage figures and finished with a round over the show fences.

"Okay!" She beamed at both of them as they rode out of the ring. "You're all set. Couldn't be better. Give the horses a day's rest before the show."

"See," Susan told Whitney. "I told you that you'd be ready."

"Yeah, you're right." Whitney grinned. "It felt good too, but I still wish we were riding in the same class."

"And compete against each other? No way. This way we can both take a first – you in novice, me in training," she joked. But even as she spoke, Susan sobered. It wasn't going to be that easy, and already she was starting to get nervous flutters in her stomach.

138

On Sunday morning Susan waited outside the starting box at the beginning of the Winter Farm cross-country trail.

"Go!" the course judge called to the rider ahead of her, and horse and rider galloped off across the field toward the first of the jumps on the rolling and winding course. Whitney had already ridden the novice course and had confided to Susan that she'd done better than she'd expected. Both Susan and Whitney had come through the dressage with flying colors, but as she guided Star into the starting box to wait for their turn, Susan knew the cross-country would be the most difficult test.

The judge checked her timer. There was a lapse of several minutes between each entrant's start, so there were normally at least two riders on the course at any one time. The starter looked up at Susan. "Ready," she said. Susan settled herself in the saddle, preparing both herself and Star. "Go!"

Susan heeled Star, and they were off toward the first rail fence. She'd walked the course twice that morning and knew what obstacles to expect, but Star didn't. He needed her guidance, and it had better be good guidance, Susan thought. They landed off the first jump. She headed him down to the end of the field, following the flats marking the course. They left the bright sunshine and entered the green shadow of the woods. Following a well-ridden trail, they went downhill to a log barrier beside a brook. Star jumped cleanly, and Susan urged him uphill over a winding course through the wood and over a rustic log spread. After that, there was a sharp left turn, then up a steep bank, over a fence at the top, a stride, then down again into a small clearing. They sailed over a pyramid of logs and stretched out on an easy gallop down a length of level road. On to a wide combination water and brush – lift, extend, land – several strides, and down a steep embankment to a stone wall. Susan sat well back in the saddle and held Star in check as they descended, and then squeezed with her legs, and they were over. Only a few more fences, but she didn't allow herself to think of the end of the course – only one fence at a time. They jumped down into a sunken roadway, out again, around a group of trees to a rustic double gate, then a long flat gallop to a set of rails, and they were out!

Only when they were past the finish judge, who had stopwatch in hand, did Susan relax. She ran her hand down Star's lathered neck and whispered words of praise in his ears. "You did a great job, boy, incredible! I'm so proud of you!"

Star nickered wearily. The course had been demanding for both of them, but as far as Susan could tell, they'd come through with no penalties. The worst part was over. She headed Star over the rolling field toward the van for a much needed rest before show jumping began.

Two hours later they finished the much simpler show-jumping course with a clean round and trotted back to happy smiles.

"Congratulations!" Mr. Holmes beamed. "I think you're leading."

"We are," Susan said breathlessly as she slid from the saddle. Her legs were shaking with relief to have it over. She hadn't really expected to win her training division – just to do well enough not embarrass her or Star.

"So far," her father said, "although all the riders haven't finished. You were clean in cross-country and show

140

jumping, third in dressage. It'll depend on who else goes clean and whether they have a better time." Her father pulled Star's saddle from his back. He was tall and slender – and Susan thought pretty handsome – in his red-jacketed dress outfit. He and Tuxedo were waiting for the advanced division of the show jumping to go off. Kirin and Joany, who were dressed and were walking their horses under the trees, were waiting for the preliminary.

"Where's Whitney?" Susan asked. Susan had been thrilled to see Whitney go clear in the novice show jumping.

"Over at the end, walking Bravo."

Before setting off with Star in that direction, Susan grabbed some carrots out of the tack box. "You sure deserve these, big guy," she said to Star. "You were wonderful!" The horse whuffed his acknowledgment, but he was definitely tired. It had been a long, hard day for both of them, with three competitions in an eight-hour period.

As they walked along the grassy aisle between horse vans, Susan saw other riders glance their way. Several smiled and called, "Good job." Susan smiled back, then saw a young rider leading his horse, a tall chestnut. She recognized him from the horse show in New York.

"Hi there," he called. "Remember me? Ronny Anderson. I just watched your round. Nice! Nice-looking horse, too," he added.

"Thanks," Susan said. She was amazed he still remembered her. "You waiting to go?" she asked.

"Yeah. We're in preliminary. How'd you do on cross-country?"

"Clean, thank goodness. How about you?" Susan knew

he would have jumped a more difficult course than she and Star had.

"Okay," Ronny answered. "We screwed up a little on the water, but all in all, okay. Is this the horse you were telling me about at the show?" he asked with interest.

"This is him," Susan smiled.

"Then you've come a long way from what you were saying."

"You think so?" Susan blushed.

"I thought you said you were just starting out?"

"Well, we were . . . together, that is."

Whitney walked up, leading Bravo. She smiled at Ronny. "Don't I know you? Madison Square Garden, right?"

"Right. Whitney, isn't it? Nice to see you again. How'd you do?"

"Okay, I guess," Whitney said. "I mean, we got over – no faults, but I'm only riding novice."

"Still –" Ronny began, when someone from his van called his name.

"Mount up!" they said.

"Time for me to go. Maybe I'll see you later," he added to both girls, but especially to Susan.

"Good luck!" Susan and Whitney told him.

"Thanks, we may need it. See ya!"

"He remembered me from the show," Susan explained to Whitney when Ronny was gone.

Whitney grinned. "After today, I think a lot of people will be remembering you and Star."

They walked the horses until the preliminary and advanced entrants had finished the show course, then went back to the van. Both Kirin and Joany looked satisfied, and Susan's father was smiling. "Overall, not bad," he said. "I think we'll get some ribbons today. Both of you girls tack up again. Looks like you'll both be called back for the presentations."

"You're kidding!" Whitney cried. "Bravo and me, too?"

"You're up with the novice leaders." Mr. Holmes winked.

"Oh, wow! I wish my parents had been here to see this!"

In the end Whitney got her blue ribbon in novice. Susan and Star took a second in intermediate, but it was a good second, only one point behind the winning horse and rider, who'd been competing together for quite a while. Susan was proud, satisfied, and happy. "This is a good start, boy," she praised Star, "a real good start!"

There was more good news. Kirin, Joany, and Mr. Holmes all placed near the top of preliminary and advanced, Mr. Holmes getting a first in advanced.

"Time to go home and celebrate," Mr. Holmes said with a laugh as they started loading up the van.

"I guess!" Whitney said.

It didn't end there. After Susan and Star took a first in training at Three Oaks two weeks later, they started seriously talking about doing well at Groton.

"The way that horse is coming along," Lyle told Susan when they returned to the farm after the competition, "you'd be fools not to go for it. I'll help you on the weekends if you want."

"We all will," Mr. Holmes said. "If everything goes well, I think you have a shot at taking the training division."

143

"Are you serious?" Susan asked, barely believing him. "All the best riders on the East Coast will be there!"

"Oh, I'm serious," her father said with Lyle nodding his agreement in the background. "You two should see yourselves when you're jumping."

Susan looked up at Star, thanking her heavenly stars for bringing him to her. "Think we can do it, big guy?" she asked quietly.

The horse nudged her and bobbed his head confidently.

"Okay, let's go for it!" Susan said with determination.

"Hey, that will look good on you," Whitney told Susan as she held up a bright, short-sleeved top that she could wear for practice during the hot summer months. Susan quickly glanced in the nearby mirror in the tack store. The color was right for her, but she still got a little shock every time she looked in a mirror. She couldn't believe how much she'd changed since the fall, or that she was now even interested in what colors she wore.

"It's on sale, too," Susan said. "I've got enough saved up from teaching. Maybe I'll buy it." The girls had finished their Saturday training early and had gone into Norbridge with Susan's mother. There weren't many stores in the small village, but because of the number of horse people in the area, there was a very decent tack shop in town. The dozen or so shops nestled in the valley were housed in converted New England clapboard buildings.

Whitney suddenly jabbed Susan with her elbow and motioned with her head to the far end of the store, where the dressing rooms were.

Susan looked over the counters displaying saddles, bridles, riding accessories, and clothing to see Tara standing in front of the big mirror outside the dressing room, admiring her reflection. She was wearing a new dress-riding outfit – boots to hard hat. Tara gave a satisfied smile and nodded to the woman at her side, who had to be her mother, since they looked so much alike. The two of them turned to the saleswoman who was hovering a few feet away.

"That'll set her back a few dollars," Whitney whispered. "Last week I looked at those boots she has on – three hundred bucks. She's going all out for Groton, isn't she? There isn't even anything wrong with her old outfit."

"I guess," Susan said, thinking that her parents could never afford gear like that for her. The outfit they'd given her for Christmas hadn't been nearly as expensive – not that she minded.

"You and Star better keep at it," Whitney said. "She's not going to ride any better with a new outfit, but she's sure serious about winning!"

"We'll keep at it, all right," Susan said with more determination than ever.

Tara went back into the dressing room to change. As soon as Susan paid for her top, Mrs. Holmes waved to them through the shop window to tell them it was time to head back.

"Keep your leg on him, Susan!" her father shouted from the side of the cross-country course. "Don't let him stop. He knows what's down there by now. Get after him!"

Susan nodded. They were practicing a water jump

146

that was giving Star trouble – a three-foot jump off level ground into shallow water. Star hadn't totally overcome his dislike of water, and in addition to that, he couldn't see beyond the drop-off. To him it was a jump into unknown territory. It took all of Susan's encouragement to get him to leap. "There's nothing to be afraid of, Star. Let's do it right this time." She held her legs hard on his sides as they approached. Still, he hesitated slightly before jumping down.

"Again!" Susan's father called.

They did it again, and again and again. Finally, on their fourth try, Star leaped smoothly down into the water, surged across and up the gently sloping bank opposite. "Good boy!" Susan praised him. "That's the way. One more time, okay? Then we'll call it quits here."

They moved on to a big, closed combination of three fences of sturdy logs. Their ends were connected to form a large triangle. The easiest way to take the jump was at the wide end of the triangle, jumping the first fence, landing, then jumping the second, like an in-and-out. But for training level Susan and Star had to jump the opposite end, clearing both fences in one huge leap. Here Susan had a problem. The size of the jump intimidated her, and she found herself backing off. Her aides to Star were weak, and he repeatedly shied out.

"It's my fault," Susan cried in frustration.

"Stop thinking of how big those logs are," Kirin yelled to her. "The fence isn't all that high or wide – just looks that way. You've jumped higher and wider fences before. Make believe the logs are flimsy little poles."

But they aren't flimsy little poles, Susan thought.

Those logs weren't going to fall in a heap if she and Star misjudged the jump. They weren't going to budge. She tried to put all thoughts of mishap from her mind, as she and Star approached for the third time. She steeled her thoughts and concentrated. *We're going over . . . it's just a little jump . . . I'll do it right this time . . . now . . . squeeze*!

She did, but Star suddenly stopped dead in his tracks, skidding to a halt with all four legs braced. Just as suddenly Susan found herself flying over his head, over the first wall of the fence, to land in a heap on the grass in the middle with her right wrist twisted under her. Immediately she felt a sharp, jabbing pain.

"Oh, no," she moaned as she rolled to her side. For a moment she didn't move. The she clasped her wrist with her left hand and pulled her feet under her. Already the wrist was throbbing and she felt faintly sick. It was the same wrist she had broken back in September.

While Kirin held Star, Whitney and Susan's father clambered over the log rails to help her.

"You all right?" her father asked worriedly.

"Yes, I think so . . . except for my wrist."

She heard Whitney groan and her father swear under his breath. "The same one?"

Susan nodded as Whitney and Mr. Holmes helped her to her feet. "What happened?" Susan cried. "Why did he stop? What did I do wrong?" Star was standing with his head down, looking through the rails at her, the picture of dejection. She felt awful, sure that it must have been her fault.

"I don't know what happened," Mr. Holmes said. "Your approach was perfect – exactly on – and this jump has never bothered him. He wasn't afraid of it – you were."

"But this time I was all set," Susan said. "Or at least I thought I was."

"You were," Kirin told her. "I think something else startled him into stopping. Did you know Maxine Wertheimer was practicing the course next door, just as you jumped?"

"So?" Mr. Holmes said. But Susan and Whitney turned to stare at each other.

"Didn't you hear her shouting at her horse?" Kirin asked. "I think Star did."

"I still don't understand," Mr. Holmes said, frowning. "Why should a shout stop him dead like that?"

"I think he remembers Maxine's voice, and it scares him."

Susan had long since told Kirin what she'd seen when Maxine had been working Star, but she'd never mentioned it to her father. She explained now.

"You're kidding," he said.

"You should have seen how badly she handled him that day." Susan said. "He was terrified, and I only saw her take him over one jump. If she rode the whole course like that . . ."

"No wonder she wasn't having any luck with him. I had no idea."

"I guess I should have told you, but after Star started doing well, I figured he'd forgotten."

"I guess not." Mr. Holmes shook his head and looked over at the big gray. "So, she did a number on you, eh?"

With Whitney and Mr. Holmes's help, Susan climbed over the rails of the closed fence, holding her wrist immobile against her chest. The pain was increasing. She had a horrible, sick feeling that she might have broken it again. Why now, just before Groton? She reached Star's side and caressed his neck with her good hand. "It's not your fault, buddy. Don't look so unhappy." Star rubbed his velvety nose against her shoulder. "I'll be okay," Susan said, though she knew that probably wasn't the truth. A cold sweat was breaking out on her forehead.

"I don't like ending a practice session on a bad note, but we've got to get some ice on that wrist. The horse looks pretty shaken too. Let's head back."

"It's not as bad as last time," their family doctor in Norbridge told Susan an hour later. "But you've badly sprained it, and with the recent trauma to the bones, you'd better keep that wrist quiet for a while. That means no riding."

"No!" Susan cried. "Even with a brace?"

"Not for a least a month."

"A month?" she gasped. She'd never be ready for Groton. She'd been hoping if she'd rested it for a week or two . . . but the doctor was looking at her sternly. "But I've got to ride!"

"If you want a wrist that's going to act up on you for the rest of your life, go ahead."

"No, I don't want that," Susan said. She knew that jumping and eventing put incredible stress on the wrist. The hands, wrists, and arms were under constant strain, guiding and controlling a thousand-plus pound animal over a course. But to have her and Star's show season over before it had barely started! She wanted to cry.

The doctor looked over at her parents. "See that she follows orders."

150

They were looking pretty disappointed too, but they nodded. "I'm sorry, Susan," Mrs. Holmes said softly. "We all had our hopes up pretty high. There'll be other shows."

"I know," Susan sighed, but she felt like someone had pulled the plug on her.

"I'm so disappointed!" Whitney said sympathetically when Susan called her with the bad news. "You guys were doing so well! I know you would have won at Groton. Oh, Susan, I'm so sorry."

"It's not just me who's losing out – it's Star. There'll be other shows, but to miss the top spring show in New England . . ."

"And Tara's been training like crazy for it, too. It looks like if anyone wins from the farm, it'll be her."

Susan suddenly drew in a breath. "Whitney, I've got an idea – a great idea! *You* can ride Star at Groton!"

"Me? Oh, no. No way. I'm not nearly as good as you. Besides, he only tries his best for you."

"He knows you're his friend, and with a little more practice you could compete at training level. You're almost there anyway."

"Susan, I'd really like to help you, but I just don't think I could do it."

Susan tried another approach. "Look, the doctor said I have to rest my wrist for a month. There's a good chance it'll be okay for Groton. I can probably ride then. But Star has to stay in training *now*. If you could just keep training him for me."

Whitney hesitated. "I suppose I could do that. You really think your wrist will be okay by then?"

"Sure." Susan wasn't sure at all, but if she could get

Whitney to start riding and training Star, Whitney might build up enough confidence to ride for Susan at Groton if she had to. Susan knew it was a sneaky move, but she couldn't give up all hope of Star competing.

"Well, okay then. And heck, maybe it'll be fun. I've always wanted to ride a horse like Star – I mean, Bravo's one in a million, but he doesn't quite have Star's talent."

"So you broke your wrist again?" Tara said cheerfully the next morning at school.

"Sprained it. It's not broken."

"But I guess you won't be able to ride, then, will you? What a shame, with all the big shows coming up."

Susan could see that Tara was positively gleeful. This was probably the best news she'd had in a long time.

"Yeah," Susan said mildly. She wasn't going to let Tara egg her on. Tara would find out soon enough that Whitney was going to ride Star instead; her competition wasn't dead yet.

"See you at the stable this afternoon," Tara said as she strolled off. "You should come watch Dickens and me, now that you won't have anything else to do. We're doing fantastic."

"News travels fast," Whitney quipped as she joined Susan.

"Tara was at the farm yesterday, don't forget."

"Did you tell her I'm going to ride Star?" Whitney's eyes twinkled.

"Nope. I thought it would be fun to surprise her."

Whitney snorted a laugh. "She'll be surprised, all right. I can't wait to see her face."

They weren't disappointed. When Tara came up the farm drive for her practice session, Whitney was riding Star out to the ring with Susan walking alongside. Tara stopped in her tracks and gaped.

"*You're* going to ride him?" she screeched.

Whitney just smiled.

Tara gritted her teeth, then stomped off to the stable. She was shaking with fury, but Whitney was one of the few people Tara didn't have the nerve to put down. With big grins Whitney and Susan went into the ring.

Star hadn't protested when Whitney had climbed in his saddle; he knew Whitney was a friend. The test would be to see if he would try his best for someone other than Susan.

Susan felt strange as she watched Whitney and Star move around the ring. This was her horse; she should be in his saddle. But there wasn't anything she could do about it if she wanted Star to be ready to compete at Groton. And if anyone was going to ride Star, she was glad it was Whitney.

Susan's mother came to watch as Whitney warmed Star up and started putting him through figures. He seemed to be going fine for Whitney. He wasn't tense.

Susan sighed. "So far, so good."

"Whitney's got good hands and a good seat," Mrs. Holmes said. "If she can get over her fear of the bigger jumps, they should work fine together." She paused. "Although I wonder if he'll put quite as much into it as he does for you."

"That's what I'm wondering too."

That night after dinner, Susan went out to Star's stall. She let herself in and talked quietly to the horse a she stroked

153

his neck. "I know you're probably wondering what's going on. If you only understood what this brace on my wrist meant. But I will be riding you again! For now, though, just try your best for Whitney. It's important to me that you compete at Groton." Star nickered as if he understood. "I want everyone to see how talented you are. Maybe my wrist will be better by then, but if it's not, and you and Whitney do well, it'll be almost as wonderful as if I were riding you myself." *Almost . . . but not quite*, Susan thought. Inside she was furious at hurting her wrist again. And horribly disappointed.

But over the next couple of weeks, Whitney made real progress. Maybe Star didn't have quite the verve and fire he did when Susan was riding, but he was putting out more than enough to jump clean and athletic courses. He did seem to understand how important it was. Tara was ripped.

It wasn't all good. There were days when Whitney had no faith at all in her own abilities, when she'd falter and end up with Star refusing a jump or popping over awkwardly.

"Oh, Susan, I'll never get it all together! I'm hopeless!" Whitney cried as she dismounted and led Star away from a rustic oxer they'd popped so badly that Whitney had slid out of the saddle on landing.

"No you're not. You can't expect everything to be perfect from the start, but it'll all come together, and look how well you got him through the water jump."

"*Coming through!*" a voice called from down the trail.

They looked back to see Tara and Dickens cantering to the oxer and flying over. "Having trouble?" she called as she landed and slowed Dickens. She hadn't missed

Whitney's look of discouragement. Stopping Dickens for a second, she looked back over her shoulder. "Well, keep at it." She smiled as she cantered off.

Whitney's dark eyes were flashing. "Now there's a good reason to keep on trying!" she said with new determination. "I'll be darned if she's going to beat me!"

"Way to go!" Susan laughed.

They'd skipped the Shepley show at the beginning of June since Whitney wasn't ready, but it was looking more and more like Whitney would be ready for Groton. Her parents came over to watch several of her practice sessions and were beaming proudly when Whitney finished up.

"Not bad, eh?" Whitney grinned.

"I'm getting so excited about this show," Mrs. Duncan said. "I wish we'd been able to see the last one. But looking at some of those jumps, I'm a little nervous."

"Didn't she go over them just fine?" Mr. Duncan asked.

"I don't always go over so great." Whitney smiled. "But don't start getting all uptight, Mom, or you'll make me nervous."

"We have faith in you – and that beautiful horse! Susan, you've done a wonderful job with both of them!"

Susan blushed and managed to mumble, "Thanks."

As busy as it was at the stable, it was just as hectic at school, with end-of-the year tests and the big class picnic coming up. Susan and Whitney often studied together after they finished practice sessions.

"Am I tired or what?" Whitney said one night at Susan's, hiding a yawn behind her hand.

Susan was feeling almost as tired, although she wasn't getting the physical workout that Whitney was. "We've

155

only got our English test left, and school will be over before Groton."

"Whew! I like school, but this year I'm glad it's nearly over. What are you wearing to the picnic tomorrow?"

"Shorts – oh, and bring or wear a bathing suit. The park's right on the Housatonic, so we'll be swimming and probably doing some canoeing."

"Canoeing!" Whitney brightened. "I definitely want to try that. Do you know how?"

"Sure, I've been out with Lyle and my parents. It's not that hard as long as the rapids aren't running fast."

The next morning dawned hot and sunny. Susan put on her bathing suit and pulled white shorts over her long tanned legs and a bright blue T-shirt over her head. She checked her hair in the mirror, fluffing it with her fingers. Thanks to Whitney, her board-straight hair now fell to her shoulders with a full-bodied sheen. Her slenderness was an asset in clothes that fit and were becoming, and the blue of her shirt made her dark-lashed eyes stand out in her face. Grabbing a towel from the bathroom, Susan hurried down to meet Whitney. "Have fun!" her mother called as she shot out the door.

"We will." Actually, Susan was glad for a day off from the training. It was almost too hot to ride anyway, and she was ready for a swim. She wasn't much interested in socializing with the kids, though she had to admit she didn't feel like a total nonentity the way she had, and the food would be good. Everyone in the class had chipped in for burgers and hot dogs, and the teachers would be bringing salads and stuff.

Whitney was wearing bright pink shorts, a wild, flowered top, big sunglasses, and a floppy hat. "You look like some kind of a movie star," Susan said with a laugh.

"I felt in a fun mood this morning," Whitney answered. "The hat won't last long once we're there, and I've got my suit on underneath."

Whitney did get a few stares as they climbed out of the Duncans' car. A couple of whistles, too. But most of the kids were used to her incredible clothes by now. The two girls joined the crowd gathered in the picnic area near the river's edge. Tree-covered mountains lifted to either side of the rippling river, and the air was scented with pine. Pretty soon Whitney flung her hat on a picnic table as she and Susan were invited to join a volleyball game – something that never would have happened to Susan nine months before. If she'd even gotten up the courage to go to a class outing, she would have hung miserably along the sidelines and been ignored.

An hour later, dripping with sweat, the players dashed into the water for a swim. Then it was lunchtime, and they flocked to the barbecue grills, the tables of food, and coolers of soda. With full plates they plopped down on the grass or at picnic tables under the big pines to eat.

"After we eat, let's go canoeing," Whitney said to Susan. "The water's not too rough. You'll have to tell me what to do, though."

"Sure. No problem. It'll be fun." Susan glanced up from her plate of potato salad to see Tara watching from the next table. Tara was wearing a bright pink bikini, and all the guys had been staring at her. Tara gave Susan a smile, then turned to talk to one of her friends.

"Tara just smiled at me," Susan whispered in astonishment to Whitney.

"Maybe she has gas," Whitney answered.

Susan strangled back a laugh. "You're awful!"

A few minutes later they slid a canoe into the shallow waters of the river. Whitney sat on the front seat, Susan on the rear. "See, it's easy," Susan said to Whitney. "Just paddle on one side. I'll paddle on the other. To turn, we both paddle on the same side, or I'll drag my oar."

"Gotcha," Whitney answered, pushing her paddle vigorously through the water. "There are a lot of rocks out here."

"The river's pretty low. We'll steer around them. Keep a lookout, though, for the ones that are just under the surface."

They weren't the only ones out on the river. All half dozen of the canoes were in use. Susan saw Tara and a friend climb into one.

"Turn right, Whitney!" she called as she saw a boulder looming ahead. "No, to go right, you paddle on the left. Whew!" she added as they missed the boulder by inches. A few seconds later Susan was yelling out directions again as they almost rammed another rock.

"This isn't as easy as you said," Whitney told her.

"Wait till we get away from these rocks. There's a nice smooth spot up ahead. Watch out!" Susan added with a yelp. Whitney pushed them away from the semi-buried log with her paddle. But they got tangled again when they finally reached the smoother water.

"There's another branch down there," Whitney said. "I can push it out of the way," she added, rising and reaching out with her paddle.

"No, Whitney! Don't stand up in a – " Susan began, when suddenly they were thumped from behind. Their canoe rocked crazily from side to side. Whitney tried to keep her balance, but it was a lost cause. She fell sideways into the water with a huge splash. Her momentum tipped the canoe to its side, and Susan tumbled in after her.

They both stood up in the chest-deep water, sputtering and dripping. Tara and her friend glided by.

"Sorry," Tara called. "We couldn't stop. Are you all right?" Both girls in Tara's canoe were barely hiding their grins.

Susan made a grab for their overturned canoe before it floated down the river. She heard hysterical laughter from the other boats behind her. "Wish I had a camera," someone yelled.

Tara started giggling then too. Whitney glared at the departing canoe. "You did that on purpose! Just wait till Groton, Tara Pendleton!" Whitney angrily pushed wet strands of hair out of her eyes. "And I lost my good sunglasses, too," she moaned, then looked over at Susan. The two girls stared at each other for a second, then burst into laughter. "What a sight," Whitney said. "But I meant what I said about Groton! Little creep."

Susan and Whitney joined in with the cheers of all the
Norbridge Regional Middle School students as they flooded
out of the doorways of the brick building on the last day of
school. "Another year finished!" Whitney cried. "And we
both managed to get decent grades – what a relief!"

"We can really concentrate on Groton from here on out,"
Susan answered.

Now, nearly two weeks later, Susan and Whitney set
out for a tour of the Groton House Farm grounds. They'd
arrived from Connecticut an hour before and had finished
walking and settling the horses in the rented stables.
Dressage competition would begin early the next morning,
with cross-country on Saturday and stadium show jumping
on Sunday. All around them were other competitors
and horses and some vans were still arriving in the late
afternoon.

"Wow!" Whitney said as they set out up the road from
the stabling and parking area. "Look at all the people! I
didn't think the show was going to be *this* big!"

"Exciting, huh?" Susan said enthusiastically.

"It's making me nervous. I'm beginning to wish your wrist was okay again and you could ride. I don't know if I'm ready for this."

Susan glanced down at the Ace bandage tightly circling her wrist, and wished the stupid thing was healed too. But she knew it wasn't right yet. She still got twinges if she used her right hand for anything heavy. But she had to buoy up Whitney. "You'll be fine, Whit, and Star's all set. You know he'll put his heart into it and get you through."

"Mmm," Whitney said. "Maybe I'll feel better after I see the course."

Susan wondered if Whitney would feel *worse* after seeing the cross-country course, but she didn't say anything. They passed the fenced area where the stadium jumping would take place, although none of the fences had been set up. They followed the lane past the stables and barns to the dressage arenas, which had been readied for the following day's competition.

They'd spotted several of the fences on the cross-country course as they'd walked. The course wound all across the farm, through wood and field, crossing the main avenue at one point. They each had a program outlining the course and the fences, but the entire course wouldn't be open for the competitors to walk until the following afternoon.

Whitney was looking increasingly uncertain as she caught glimpses of the few visible fences. Susan knew she was going to have to give her friend a pep talk, but if Whitney and Star did well in dressage in the morning – and Susan was sure they would – Whitney would start feeling more confident.

The two girls turned and followed the road back to the stabling area. There seemed to be even more people milling around.

"Hey, there's Maxine Wertheimer," Whitney said as they passed an especially sleek van.

"I saw her listed in the program," Susan said. "But she's not in your division – she's riding in the first junior training. You're in the second."

"Wait till she sees the horse she thought was a loser." Whitney forgot her worries for a moment and smiled.

"If she even watches."

"Oh, I bet she will. Have you seen Tara yet?"

"She was coming with her parents, but I haven't seen her. Don't worry. We'll know when she gets here." Since the school picnic Tara had barely spoken to Susan and Whitney, but she'd been doing plenty of bragging around the stables. Susan wondered if Tara would be as confident when she saw the quality of the horses and riders at Groton.

The Holmeses and the Duncans were staying at a nearby motel during the meet. Unlike at other shows, only Whitney and Star and Tara and Dickens were competing from Shadowbrook Farm. The others were waiting for the following weekend, when the course and competition would be more difficult.

"So, what did you think?" Mr. Holmes asked Whitney when the girls returned.

"I'm almost afraid to see the cross-country. It looks scary."

"It won't be as bad as you think. Don't worry." Then he added to his wife and the Duncans, "Is everybody about ready to head out for some dinner?"

162

"Just let me check on Star before we go," Susan said. "Whitney, you want to come with me?"

The two girls hurried over to the nearby stabling. Every one of the temporary stalls was taken, and Star and Dickens were stabled near the end. They saw Tara coming out of Dickens' stall. She locked the stall door and was brushing bits of bedding from her jeans when she turned and saw them. For a second her eyes narrowed. Then she gave them a quick nod and walked off.

"I can't believe she didn't make any nasty comments," Whitney said. "I wonder if she's getting nervous."

"She probably is. Remember how uptight she was before the Hunt Club show?"

"I don't blame her if she's uptight now," Whitney said as Susan unlatched Star's stall, and she and Whitney went inside.

The big gray was delighted to see them. He whickered happily and walked over to rub his head against Susan's arm. "Yeah," Susan said, scratching his ears. "You're not used to this place, are you? We'll be back to check you after dinner and start braiding your mane. How's your hay and water?"

"Fine," Whitney said. "I just checked." She came over to rub the other side of Star's neck. The horse whuffed out sweet breaths of appreciation. "You're going to help me tomorrow, aren't you?" Whitney added. "I'm going to be a wreck."

Star gave her a soft look as if to say, "Of course."

"We'll be back later," Susan told him. "Take a snooze and relax."

After dinner in town, Mr. Holmes and Mr. Duncan drove

the girls back over to the stables for an hour. While the girls carefully combed and braided Star's mane for his dressage performance, Mr. Holmes and Mr. Duncan strolled along the stables, looking over the other horses and chatting with people Mr. Holmes knew from other events. "That looks pretty good," Whitney said when they had the last braid secured. "I just hope he doesn't go rolling in his bedding tonight."

Susan was studying the finished product. "I'm not sure I like the braids. Maybe I'm just not used to them."

"They look great," Whitney told her. "Right, Star?"

He tossed his head and snorted and immediately stepped over to his hay net.

"I don't think he's impressed." Whitney laughed.

Mr. Holmes and Mr. Duncan had stopped outside the stall.

"Ready?" Mr. Holmes asked. "You have to be up early."

"Ready. See you in the morning," Susan said dropping a kiss on Star's nose.

"So what did you think of the competition?" Susan asked her father.

"Good horses, good riders. I see Star's former owner is riding in junior training."

"A different division, but have you seen her horse? I haven't had a chance."

"I saw him in the stall, a nice-looking Anglo-Arab. Barry Jenkins owned and trained him before, so he's well conditioned and experienced."

"I guess she expects to win this weekend, then," Whitney said gloomily.

"Star's just as good and so are you!" Susan said quickly.

"You know how Maxine handles her horses – they don't exactly love her for it."

"Just relax, Whitney," Mr. Duncan said. "There's no point in making yourself sick worrying about things before they happen."

Whitney gave her father a watery smile. "I know. You're right, Pop."

"Susan, you awake?" Whitney whispered from the other bed in the motel room they shared. It was four in the morning.

"Yes. I can't sleep any more."

"Me neither. I keep thinking of that cross-country course."

"That's tomorrow, Whit."

"I still keep thinking about it."

"Wait till you walk the course this afternoon and get a good look at the jumps. It won't seem so bad."

"I'm getting up and getting my gear together."

So the two of them sat in the lamplight, carefully sorting and repacking Whitney's dressage outfit and talking until the first pink dawn light streamed through the windows. Then they dressed in shorts and T-shirts and knocked on their parents' doors.

They all had breakfast in the motel dining room, though Whitney and Susan could only pick at their food. *This is weird*, Susan thought. *I'm as much a wreck as Whitney. You'd think I was riding today.*

The stable area was already humming at six thirty, when they arrived. Horses were out of their stalls, being walked and groomed. Riders and helpers scurried around,

165

collecting brushes, towels, and tack from their individual tack boxes.

"I can't find my martingale!" someone cried.

"Darn it, where's the hoof oil? Maggie did you borrow it? Well, give it back!"

The activity wasn't surprising. The first dressage division went off at seven thirty, with eight minutes between competitors. Whitney and Star had plenty of time before they went into the arena to compete just after ten.

Star whinnied happily when they arrived at his stall. Dickens' stall was open, and Tara was already inside grooming him. She'd be riding in the same division as Whitney and Star, and she was as eager to get started as she'd been at the Hunt Club.

Susan and Whitney immediately set to work finishing Star's grooming. His mane braids were still neat. Now Susan combed out his long, flowing tail while Whitney curried him.

"You don't have to do all this," Susan told Whitney. "I can finish grooming him."

"I'd rather be busy," Whitney answered. "That way I don't think so much."

Susan understood. Both of them went to work on Star with brushes, then soft cloths to pull the last flecks of dirt from his dappled coat. Susan cleaned his hoofs and applied oil so they shone; then they covered him with a light sheet to protect their work.

It was eight o'clock and already warm. "I'm going to get his tack from the van," Whitney said. "Then I'll change into my dressage outfit."

Susan nodded and Whitney hurried off. Susan realized

166

she was dying of thirst. There was a refreshment stand up near the end of the stabling – it wouldn't take her a minute to get an orange juice. Star was happily munching on some hay, and Tara was still at work in the next stall. Susan dug in her pocket and found a crumpled dollar bill, then set off along the line of stables, weaving around horses and riders. There was already a long line at the stand. Susan almost turned around and left, but this was the last chance she'd have for a while. Finally she was served a large orange juice, and she gulped it down as she headed back to Star's stall. She didn't want Whitney to be left alone and have time to get nervous, although their parents would be arriving soon.

Whitney was standing outside Star's stall, looking like a wreck, when Susan arrived. "Where have you been?" she cried as soon as she saw Susan.

"What's wrong?" Susan said instantly. Whitney looked like she had more than a simple case of nerves.

"It's Star! I went to take him out of the stall to tack him up, but he won't let me near him!"

"What?" Susan cried.

"He tried to bite me!" Whitney said in amazed horror.

"I don't believe it." Susan already had the stall unlatched and was slipping inside. "It's me, boy," she called into the semidarkness. "What's the matter? Easy, easy," she added as Star snorted nervously and backed as far as he could against the rear wall. "That's a boy," she soothed as she inched closer. "It's only me. Come on. You never get this nervous before shows. What's wrong?"

Star flicked his ears back and forth and huffed anxiously through widened nostrils. He tossed his head uncertainly.

Susan kept talking to him, inching closer. Finally he responded to her familiar voice and let her take his halter and rub her hand gently down his neck. But he was trembling.

"It's okay," Susan said gently. Her thoughts were racing. What could have happened to make him behave like this? Was he sick? He didn't feel feverish, and he'd had a great appetite that morning. She just didn't understand.

Gradually, talking to him and soothing him, she got him out of the stall. Whitney handed her a lead shank, then stepped back a few feet. Her dark eyes were wide and confused. Star flung up his head, snorted, and looked all around, then pranced uneasily.

"Easy, easy," Susan said again. She noticed Tara and Dickens were gone, probably out to the practice ring. Susan just couldn't understand what had happened to turn Star into a jittering, overexcited ball of nerves.

"He – he was like this when I came back." Whitney uncharacteristically stuttered. "I didn't do anything."

"Of course you didn't." Then Susan saw Tara returning, leading Dickens. "Did anything happen to Star while I was gone?" Susan quickly demanded.

Tara had already noticed Star's condition, and her fair brows shot up in real surprise. "Not that I know of," Tara answered. "His old owner came by for a minute . . . Maxine Wertheimer. That's all. She was real nice. She talked to me, then said she was interested in seeing how her old horse was coming along. She didn't think anyone would mind if she went in to take a look at him."

"You let her go into his stall?" Susan exclaimed.

Tara shrugged. "Well, why not?"

Susan couldn't really blame Tara. Tara didn't know anything about the way Maxine had handled Star in the past, and that he was afraid of her. But Susan knew now why Star was acting like he was.

Susan and Whitney's parents arrived at that moment and Susan's parents immediately knew something was wrong. Her father gave Susan a questioning look. Quietly Susan explained.

Whitney was close to tears. "Susan, I can't ride him when he's like this. I'm scared and he'll know it! I'll never be able to get him to relax and do a good job. We'll make a mess of everything! You're the only one who can calm him down. You've got to ride instead of me. Please!"

Susan looked at her friend, then at her parents and the Duncans, who were gazing worriedly at their daughter. Mrs. Duncan came over and put an arm around Whitney's shoulders.

"Well, you *could* ride, Susan," her father finally said. "If you feel up to it, that is. It's been a month since you hurt your wrist. Of course, you haven't ridden in a month either. It's up to you. Otherwise we'll pull him out of competition. It would be insanity for Whitney to ride when both she and the horse are upset."

Susan didn't have to think – she knew instantly what she wanted to do. "I'll ride," she said. Even if it meant hurting her wrist again, she was going to give Star his chance.

Everyone nodded their agreement. "Susan, I'm really sorry," Whitney said tearfully. Susan handed Star's reins to her father and went over to hug her friend.

"It's okay. And Star and I will do okay."

"Well, we'd better get hopping, then," Mr. Holmes

169

said. "He needs to be tacked up, warmed up. You've got to change – but you didn't bring your riding gear, did you?" He suddenly realized.

"Whitney and I are the same size. I can wear hers."

"Your mother can go up and let the show committee know that you're the official rider. Okay, let's go."

Star still looked like he was ready to jump out of his skin, but Susan's father took him away from the commotion and walked him while Susan rushed off to the van with Whitney to change into Whitney's dressage outfit. Whitney was full of apology.

"I'm letting you down," she said. "I know we were hoping you'd ride all along, but you haven't had a chance to practice."

"But I know how to do everything. Don't worry, Whit." Susan gave her friend a smile. "I'm glad I'm riding."

Less than an hour later Susan, in Whitney's crisp black-and-white dressage outfit, an Ace bandage wrapped tightly around her wrist, mounted Star and rode him into the practice ring. He was skittish, looking everywhere, ready to shy. Susan just hoped she could get him to relax in time for their turn in the dressage arena. "Easy, boy," she whispered to him. "It's me up here now. Your old owner isn't going to get near to you again, even if I have to sleep in your stall. We've done all this before. We can do it again. And you know that you can trust me."

Star's ears flicked back as he listened, and her soft words seemed to be getting through to him as she took him through some warm-up figures. Slowly he began to concentrate, forget the distractions around them, and

170

respond to Susan's aides. Susan felt ready, but she knew it would still be touch and go with Star.

It was their turn in the arena. Susan tried to still her fluttering stomach and ignore the crowd of spectators. She had to concentrate fully too. They entered the ring at a sitting trot and stopped to salute the judges. Then she started Star through the test. Susan put everything from her mind except the exercises they had to perform. She felt a wave of relief when Star responded perfectly as they walked, trotted, and cantered through the required figures in the rectangular ring. Star changed gaits at the barest touch of Susan's heel and rein, stopped on a dime and performed beautiful extensions at the walk and trot. As Susan stopped and saluted the judges at the conclusion of their test, her heart was pounding with relief. *One down, two to go*, she thought.

Happy smiles and congratulations from the Holmeses and Duncans met Susan and Star when they returned. "I'm so glad you rode!" Whitney said. "You two looked amazing! He just does something special for you that he doesn't do for anyone else."

Susan reached up, rubbed Star's nose, and gave him a kiss.

That afternoon they walked the undulating cross-country course, Mr. Duncan offering to stay behind and keep a watch on Star's stall. They weren't going to take any chances at having the horse upset again.

"You're going to have to watch your approach here," Mr. Holmes told Susan at a big corner fence, "and watch your striding to this oxer. You can do it in two, but your angle's better if you swing out a little and put in the extra stride. It shouldn't cost you much in time."

Susan nodded, trying to memorize the difficult spots and judge the best approach to each obstacle. She felt a lot more apprehensive walking the course, knowing she would be riding the fences. There were some tough parts, but nothing she and Star couldn't handle if they were working as a team. Not that it was going to be easy on either of them. Susan glanced down at her wrist. The dressage had hardly bothered it at all. She hoped the same would be true for the far more strenuous cross-country.

"I think that coffin ditch might claim a few riders," Mrs. Holmes said when they'd finished walking the entire course for the second time. "Be on your toes and keep after him, but you two can handle this course. I'm sure of it."

"Thanks, Mom." Susan smiled, but her smile was wobbly. She was getting nervous.

"How much longer?" Susan asked Whitney late the following morning. She and Star had just finished their cross-country warm-up, and she was walking Star under the trees not far from the start of the course. He was himself again, relaxed and concentrating, recovered from his encounter with his former owner.

"Fifteen minutes," Whitney said.

The first junior training division had finished. Susan had heard that Maxine Wertheimer had gone clean. Now Tara was going off, and Mr. Holmes had gone with her to the starting box. Tara and Dickens had done well in dressage but were two points behind Susan and Star, who had come through with no penalties. That morning Tara had appeared tense with determination to outdo Susan on cross-country.

"She's off," Whitney said, but Susan was barely listening. She was mentally preparing herself for the test ahead. Three more riders went off at two-minute intervals.

"Mount up," Susan's mother told her.

Susan nodded, pulled down Star's stirrups, gave Star a quick hug, then mounted. "Okay, big guy, here we go."

"Part of me is going to be riding the course with you," Whitney said. "Good luck, buddy."

Susan's parents and the Duncans echoed her good luck wishes. Susan fastened the chin strap on her cross-country helmet, adjusted the numbered vest tied over her short-sleeved shirt, and smoothed the wrist-length gloves she wore for added grip on the reins. Star was already fitted out with leather boots to protect his shins. They were ready.

She walked Star to the starting box and took several deep, steadying breaths. Star was on his toes as they approached the box. His neck was arched and his ears pricked forward. He knew what was coming.

"We can do this together, boy," Susan whispered. "I know you'll do your best for me."

Star bobbed his head. Susan faced him toward the open end of the box, then readied herself, muscles poised, shoulders straight, head up with her eyes looking between Star's ears. The starter called, "Go!"

Susan gave Star leg, and he instantly surged forward over the open field toward the first obstacle. They easily cleared the vertical slab fence, then galloped into a long curve in the trail toward a rustic oxer. Squeeze, soar, land, and Star was over with both height and extension. Susan slowed their pace crossing the avenue, then picked up some speed again along a wooded trail that ended with a jump over a logjam. Seconds later they galloped out into an open field close to the stabling area, where a lot of spectators were gathered.

Star started for a moment at the sight of the crowd,

but Susan quickly checked him with the reins to get his attention and he galloped on smoothly. They approached another big oxer. Susan checked her line, gathered Star slightly, squeezed with her legs, and they were over. They circled the field back toward the avenue to a corner jump. Star flew over at a perfect angle and landed, and Susan put in the extra stride her father had suggested as she turned Star sharply left toward the next obstacle. *One, two, three, squeeze,* she thought. Star lifted like a bird. In a corner of Susan's mind it registered that Star was performing better than he ever had before. He was putting everything into his jumps; his long strides were eating up the rolling, winding course. But this wasn't the time to grow overly confident. They had a long way to go.

Downhill they sailed to the bullfinch, a huge brush, then around to the coffin ditch, appropriately named, Susan thought. She brought Star in carefully, gathering his strides with pressure on the reins, then lined up to the fence to their side of the ditch and gave Star enough leg and rein to lift and extend over the first fence. Leaning back as they came down the bank, Susan gave him leg again as they jumped the ditch, then surged up to the second fence at the top of the opposite bank, he stretched himself over. Susan felt like they were airborne. Then they landed, and already she was looking ahead to the next obstacle not far ahead. The obstacles weren't equal distances apart; some entailed long gallops; others were separated by only a few strides.

They neatly cleared the next big gate, then galloped up the length of another field toward a triangular stack of railroad ties. Susan squeezed hard, and Star cleared the obstacle with room to spare. They circled around near the dressage arena toward a heavily wooded stretch of trail. Star lifted smoothly through a rustic in and out – over, land, squeeze, jump – around and into the long and winding course through the woods. Susan adjusted her eyes to the dappled green shadows, then readied Star for a jump over a set of horizontal logs. He landed smoothly; then they were off through a narrow stretch of shaded trail to a triangular coop. The dirt of the trail was damp, and it churned as they worked their way out of the woods. Susan slowed Star's pace slightly, but soon enough they were into the clear again and heading toward a rugged set of beams. After that was the water jump.

Star didn't hesitate for an instant as Susan urged him down the slope into the belly-deep water, across the water-filled log enclosure, then encouraged him to make a strong jump up onto the bank. Susan refused to let herself think that there were only two more fences. She refused to speculate on their time, or to feel satisfied that so far they'd gone clean with no run-outs or refusals from Star. She headed Star toward the descending combination jump, then a brisk gallop across an open meadow toward another big coop, around sharply to the left, and a short gallop to the finish.

With a sigh of relief Susan sat back in the saddle, dropping Star into a canter, then a trot, patting his sweat-drenched neck, praising him. "Way to go, Star! Incredible! I love you!"

Her parents, the Duncans, and Whitney hurried over, "How'd it go?" they asked in one breath. The long course was spread out over such varying terrain that there was no way anyone could see more than a few of the jumps at a time.

"We went clean!" Susan beamed, unsnapping her chin strap. As she did, she felt a twinge in her wrist. She hadn't noticed it while she was riding, but it definitely hurt now. Whitney held Star's reins as Susan dismounted. "How do you think our time was?" she asked breathlessly.

"Well within the optimum," her mother said. "I'd say you had the best round so far in this division."

Susan felt slightly dazed. She'd been concentrating so intently, she needed a few minutes to take everything in. She tried to clear her head as they all trooped back toward the stabling area. Star was a little tired from his exertions, but not overly so. With a good sponge-down, a walk and a rest, he'd be fine for the next day's show jumping. Susan wasn't so sure about herself. Her wrist throbbed, but she didn't say a word to anyone.

"One sad piece of news," Mr. Holmes said. "Tara had a run-out and a double refusal near the end of the course. She and Dickens were eliminated."

"She must be disappointed," Susan said, knowing how she'd feel if she and Star had been eliminated.

"Furious is more like it," Whitney answered.

Back at the stabling area, Susan and Whitney lavishly sponged Star down, at which he whickered his appreciation, then took him for a long walk to cool him out. Susan would walk him again that night to keep his muscles from stiffening, and give him a good brushing that would also work to massage his muscles.

Mr. Holmes had already looked the horse over carefully, checking for any heat in his legs, but Star had come through in fine shape.

Susan put a sheet over him, gave him a well-deserved bran mash, refilled his hay and water buckets, and hugged his neck before leaving the stall. It was almost like a dream to think of how far they'd come. What would she have done without him? "Thanks, boy," she whispered. "You're wonderful. I love you so much."

Star rubbed his head against her and whickered contentedly.

Susan was beginning to feel the aftermath of her exertions. Now that her adrenaline level was back to normal, she was noticing the ache in her wrist more and more, and she suddenly felt exhausted. Maybe food would help. She and Whitney headed toward the refreshment stand and nearly collided with Tara, who was coming the other way.

"I'm sorry about your elimination, Tara," Susan said.

Tara just glared at her. "Sure you are," she snipped. "It's the best thing that could have happened as far as you're concerned. And it wasn't fair anyway. There was a shadow across the jump. Dickens couldn't see what he was doing! I had a clear round until then!"

"It was really bad luck," Susan said.

Tara made a growling noise in her throat and strode off.

"Whew!" Susan said. "She's really a poor loser, isn't she? She wasn't the only one eliminated."

"She wasn't the only one who had to jump into shadow, either," Whitney added. "And there were a couple of bad falls. At least she got through without hurting herself or her horse."

That evening, when they returned to walk Star, they checked the bulletin board at the headquarters building for the final day's standings. They had to wait their turn, since there were obviously a lot of interested riders.

When they finally squeezed through, Whitney was the first to give a stifled shout. "You're tied for first!" she yelped. "Oh, my gosh, but I knew you'd do well!"

"I am?" Susan gasped. "Who am I tied with?"

Whitney turned to her and gave a flashing-toothed smile. "Oh, just Maxine Wertheimer."

Susan's head jerked up. She stepped back out of the way of the other riders waiting to see the scores and took a deep breath. "Maxine! I don't believe it. But she's won some open intermediate and advanced trials."

"Not with this horse." Whitney continued smiling. "This ought to be very interesting!"

As they walked away from the headquarters building, Susan heard her name called. "Hey, Susan. I just saw the results. Good going!"

It was Ronny Anderson, and he walked over with a big grin. "Looks like you're going places with that horse!"

"Thanks. I didn't know you were riding. I mean, I haven't seen you anywhere."

"Easy not to see someone in this crowd," he answered. "I'm here giving my younger brother a little coaching. I'll be riding in open intermediate next weekend, but I walked this course. It wasn't easy. You did really well to go clean without any penalties."

He walked with them as Susan and Whitney headed back to the stables, where they were meeting Mr. Holmes. They talked about the show, the courses, various riders, and horses. Mr. Holmes was already waiting when they reached Star's stall. Susan made introductions.

"I know your father from the show circuit," Mr. Holmes said. "How's he doing?"

"He's breeding and training now," Ronny said. "I'm the one who's trying to keep up the family's riding reputation," he said smiling. "Well, I'll let you go. I'll be there to watch you jump tomorrow," he added to Susan. "Good luck."

All the while they'd been talking, Susan was aware of the throbbing in her wrist, but it wasn't until she and Whitney were back in their motel room that she confided to Whitney that it was bothering her.

"Oh, no," Whitney groaned. "You don't think it's broken again or anything?"

Susan shook her head. "It would hurt more than this if it was. But it's not right."

"I'll go down to the office and get some ice," Whitney said, and shot out the door. A few minutes later she returned with a bucketful of cubes. "Let me get a towel. Maybe if you keep it wrapped in ice, it'll be okay by morning." Whitney disappeared into the bathroom and returned a moment later with an ice-filled towel. Meanwhile Susan had undressed and put on the long T-shirt she wore as a summer nightgown. She felt totally exhausted.

Whitney wrapped the compress around Susan's wrist and secured it with one of her own silk scarves.

"Whitney!" Susan protested. "That's a designer scarf."

"Yeah, so? I can get more. Your wrist's more important right now. It wouldn't be hurting if I hadn't turned chicken!"

Susan sighed and sagged back against the pillows. She was too tired to argue. Even the pain in her wrist couldn't keep her awake.

When she woke up in the morning, her wrist did feel better. Whitney must have taken off the compress before she'd gone to bed – Susan wasn't met with a bed full of soggy towels. Whitney was still asleep as Susan got up, dressed in jeans and another T-shirt, and wrapped the Ace bandage around her wrist. *I'll be okay*, she thought. *Star and I will make it through. We have to – we're in first!*

That morning Whitney saw Susan wince a couple of times as they groomed Star. As soon as they were through, Susan put more ice on her wrist. "Just don't tell my parents!" Susan whispered to Whitney. "I have to ride, and if they know my wrist is bothering me, they won't let me."

Whitney nodded silently.

Now Susan was in her dress habit, waiting to enter the show ring. The stadium jumping was done in reverse order of finish in the earlier events. Since Susan and Star were tied for first, they'd jump second to last, before the first-place finisher in the earlier junior-training division, Maxine.

Star was in good shape. He hadn't shown any stiffness that morning when Susan had walked him and carefully studied his movements. He'd eaten a good breakfast, too, but then he had stayed in condition over the last month. She was the one whose muscles were slightly sore from not having ridden. But it was her wrist that worried her. She prayed it wouldn't give out on her before the show jumping was finished.

It was to her and Star's advantage to jump close to last. They could watch the other competitors, see how the course was riding, discover at which fences horses and riders were having difficulty, and know what to correct before they got into the ring.

The last rider before Susan left the ring with one knockdown and one refusal. So far no one had gone clean without time penalties. Susan readied herself as she heard her parents', the Duncans', and Whitney's calls of good luck. Earlier she'd seen Ronny Anderson sitting in the bleachers, and he had given her a thumbs-up.

"Okay, Star," she said. "Let's do it. Clean round. We're going to have to cut one stride off the corner between the combination and the wall if we're going to do it within the allowed time."

Star's ears were back, listening to her every word. She could tell from the tension in his body that he was ready. They rode into the ring. Susan stopped and nodded to the judges, then she put every unnecessary thought from her mind, heeled Star into a canter, circled, and looked in the direction of the first jump.

Her wrist was already starting to hurt by the second jump. She willed the pain away and concentrated only on pacing Star's strides, finding perfect takeoff points, squeezing, stretching with him as he leaped, landing, looking ahead to the next jump. After having watched so many competitors jump the course, she didn't have to think about the route; she had it stamped into her mind. If she could only get through before her wrist gave out! Star seemed to have a direct channel to her mind and her pain, and he was making it easier for her. If she was even slightly off on takeoff, he corrected. His lift and extension over the jumps was incredible. Not for one second was he distracted as Susan guided him through the course. They cleared the last big fence to loud applause. They'd done the course clean and in good time! The only way they could lose now would be if Maxine went clear in better time.

182

Susan was in real pain now. She let her hand hang down limply from her side, trying to relieve the stress on her wrist, but she didn't mention her hurt wrist to her parents or Whitney, who were excitedly praising her round. With what concentration she had left, she watched Maxine's ride.

She was going clean – and in good time. *She's going to beat us*, Susan thought. *After all this, she's going to beat us*. Then, at the very last fence, Maxine must have relaxed too much – her horse didn't have quite enough lift. His rear hoofs just barely caught the rail on landing and sent it down.

Susan sat numbly amazed for a moment. She and Star had won. They'd won! It hadn't even entirely sunk in when the announcer called the finalists into the ring.

"Go on!" Whitney shouted. "You won!"

"Get out there!" her parents cried.

"Let's go, boy," Susan mumbled. Star pricked his ears and snorted excitedly. He lifted his feet high as they walked to the center of the course and lined up with the other finalists for the presentation of the ribbons. Susan was aware of Maxine Wertheimer sitting astride her own horse next to Susan as the second place finisher. She could almost feel the stab of Maxine's angry stare, but Star himself didn't really seem to react to her. Susan hoped that by now he knew that Susan would never let Maxine hurt him again. Then the judge attached the first-place ribbon to Star's bridle. "Congratulations!" She smiled. "Lead out the victory gallop!"

Susan weakly smiled back. This was a wonderful moment, but Susan wondered if she had the stamina left to finish a gallop around the ring. She heeled Star forward, and the other top finishers followed as they raced over the grass to applause from the spectators. Susan saw Ronny waving and cheering for her, but by the time they'd circled half the course, the pain in Susan's wrist was shooting straight to her brain. Every other muscle in her body felt weak because of it. She prayed for the end of the gallop, her hands lax on the reins. Star was the only one carrying them through.

Finally they rode out of the ring, toward the jubilant congratulations of Susan's parents, Whitney, and the Duncans. Susan stopped Star in front of them, then passed out cold in the saddle.

"Susan . . . come on, sweetheart . . ." She heard a voice calling, her mother's voice. Her eyes flickered open, and she looked up to see what seemed like dozens of eyes staring down at her. In fact it was only her mother and father, Whitney, Mr. and Mrs. Duncan, and Ronny Anderson.

For a second she couldn't remember where she was or what had happened. She shook her head a little to clear it.

"Thank heavens," her mother breathed. "Here, let me have that ice, Mitch. Why did you faint? The heat? Are you all right?" Her parents were talking at the same time. Susan looked over to see Star watching her from a few feet away. The blue ribbon on his bridle was fluttering in the breeze, and suddenly she remembered everything and felt a rush of joy. She smiled. "Hey, we did it, buddy . . . didn't we? What's next? Ledyard?"

Star tossed his head so his silky mane flew, then whinnied his approval.

"All right!" Susan sighed. Then she lifted her wrist to her mother. "Put the ice on here, Mom."